I0621853

BIGFOOT AWAKENED: CARNAGE

ALEX LAYBOURNE

SEVERED PRESS
HOBART TASMANIA

BIGFOOT AWAKENED: CARNAGE

Copyright © 2018 Alex Layboune
Copyright © 2018 by Severed Press

WWW.SEVEREDPRESS.COM

All rights reserved. No part of this book may be
reproduced or transmitted in any form or by any
electronic or mechanical means, including
photocopying, recording or by any information and
retrieval system, without the written permission of
the publisher and author, except where permitted by law.
This novel is a work of fiction. Names,
characters, places and incidents are the product of
the author's imagination, or are used fictitiously.
Any resemblance to actual events, locales or persons,
living or dead, is purely coincidental.

ISBN: 978-1-925711-99-8

All rights reserved.

CHAPTER ONE

The scream shattered the silence of the empty house, echoing through the large space, which only served to amplify the girl's initial terror.

"What the fuck, you scared the shit out of me," Jamie cried out as she spun to face her boyfriend, slapping him playfully on the arm.

"Woah, you kiss your mother with that mouth?" Colin, her boyfriend of four years, said with a wicked grin on his face.

"Not anymore, but I do kiss other things." It was her turn to have a mischievous smile as Colin stared at her.

"What's gotten into you?" he asked. "Not that I'm complaining."

Jamie looked around before answering. The living room was empty. All traces of the memories built up over the past 18 years were gone, the lives lived, and the lessons learned boxed up and loaded into the back of a moving van.

"I don't know, it just seems like a good time for a fresh start; find a new me that I can grow into." She smiled and wrapped her arms around her boyfriend. "I love you."

"I love you too," he replied, his lips meeting hers. He could feel her heat and knew what she wanted. "Babe, we can't, we're already late."

His argument was weak and his protestations were more for show, but they both knew he was right. Besides, the movers were coming to collect the rest of the garden furniture and the stuff in the garage. They could arrive at any time, and while she was looking for a way to change her character, becoming an exhibitionist was not on the top five things she had considered.

"Fine, but once we reach the cabin, I'm rocking your world." She smiled, and her green eyes seemed to glow with naughty intent.

"You're on. Now say your goodbyes, and I'll throw your stuff in the car." Colin kissed her on the cheek and walked away.

Alone, the emotions surprised Jamie. There was the realization that she will never step foot in the house again, the house where she grew up, the place where she learned about life and loss. Her grandfather had passed away in the upstairs bedroom; her brother had been born in it the following spring. She turned in a slow circle, looking at the shading on the wall, spots where until that week photos had been plastered, lauding every aspect of her life and her brother's.

She heard Colin slam the car doors, and a few moments later, the engine turned over. She knew he was eager to get on the road, but he would have to wait. She wasn't ready. Not just yet. Walking through the house, she ran her hand over the wall and stared at the impressions on the floor from where her mother's china cupboard had been. To this day, she could still remember the telling off she got when her friend Rosie had accidentally broken one of the plates. It had been during her seventh birthday party. Her mother had been so upset by it. She never understood why, not until she was older and heard the stories behind the items in the cupboard; the family history associated with each piece. They were all gone now, packed away in boxes with the rest of her life.

With her and Tony both going to college, her parents had decided to move to another town also, trading their suburban home for a nicer property on the coast. It was only a short flight away, but Jamie still couldn't see why they had to do everything so fast.

Walking up the stairs, she looked left, down at her parents' room, and then just before it, the bathroom. The linen closet, whose folding doors were opened outwards, exposed the empty insides, like a cadaver put out on display at the end of an autopsy. Everything of importance was removed, leaving just the shell.

Her room was at the opposite end of the hall. The door was closed, but she couldn't leave without taking one last look. Jamie knew she was being stupid and overly sentimental, but that was just who she was. Outside, she heard Colin honk the horn of his Toyota, two short sharp blasts, the same way he had done every time he came to pick her up for school, or for a date.

Her room looked much larger now that everything had been taken away, but so much had happened between those four walls; the tantrums and the sulks, the sleepovers with school friends and as she got older, with Colin. She had lost her virginity in that room, and now, it was just being discarded. She had no place to come home to, to get away from the college world for a while. Sure, she could visit her parents. They were rich enough to pay the airfare whenever she wanted it, but it would not be the same.

She blinked back a tear and shook her head, realizing even she could go too far with her nostalgic view of things.

With a heavy sigh, she walked back downstairs and out through the front door. Locking it, she popped her key through the letterbox. Her parents would be along later that day to organize the final departure, but she and her friends would be long gone, heading away for a weekend break in the mountains.

"You okay?" Colin asked, his irritation dissipating the moment he saw the emotion etched into her features.

"Yeah, I'm just being silly," she replied, wiping her eyes. "Let's get going; otherwise, we are going to be late."

They pulled away and Jamie forced herself to not look in the mirror. *It's just a house*, she told herself, yet she couldn't help but chance a look back just before they turned out of the street. It's strange because now that she had left, it really was just a house, and watching it disappear from view elicited nothing from her.

"Let's collect Tony first. He'll feel better being in the car with just us for a while." She placed her hand on Colin's thigh and flashes him a smile.

"You're the boss," Colin replies, flicking the control on the side of the wheel to browse through his Spotify playlist.

"Ugh, really?" Jamie says when Linkin Park starts playing.

"Hey, it's a classic, and I'm driving so I pick the music." The car picked up speed and as Colin started drumming on the wheel, while Jamie turned her eyes to the world zipping by just beyond the window. She was soon lost not to a daydream, but to the comforting nothingness of zoning out.

***

Tony Gardner checked his watch. They were ten minutes late to collect him, which, under normal circumstances, would have sent his world into a minor spin, but it was his sister he was waiting on, and years of experience had taught him that she would most likely even be late to her own funeral.

Still, the nerves were beginning to build, and his foot had started to tap on the pavement, an act that seemed to have irritated the man standing beside him.

Tony checked his watch again. Eleven minutes later, he let out a long, drawn-out breath when suddenly the car appeared around the corner.

The window opened, and Colin's head appeared through the hole left behind. "Did you call for a taxi?"

Tony liked Colin but didn't always get his sense of humor. He was happy when Jamie jumped out of the passenger seat and ran around to give him a hug.

She squealed as he closed his arms around her. "Oh, I missed you. How are you? How's college?"

Tony smiled and nodded, lowering his gaze to the floor. "College is good. It's fun. There's always a lot going on, and the people are cool." He raised his gaze when he was finished speaking and saw his sister smiling at him.

"I knew you would like it out there. You should stay in touch more though. I mean, it only takes a few minutes to send your favorite sister an email."

"You're my only sister," Tony stated.

"Doesn't change what I said." Jamie giggled and hurried around to the back of the car. "Dump your stuff in the trunk and get in. We've just got to pick up Stella and Ricky and then we are on the road to a weekend of freedom."

From inside the car, Colin gives a clap and a shout of agreement.

"Stella and Ricky?" Tony asks. "I thought it was just us in the car."

He stiffens at the thought of having two people in the back seat with him. Stella was cool. She had been friends with his sister for as long as he could remember, but Ricky, he had only met the man twice and didn't like him either time.

"Yeah, we had to change plans. Tammy is heading up in her own car but had to pick up a friend of hers, Susan. You're going to like Susan, but anyway, they are coming in from out of town, so it made more sense for us to head up as one group. Come on, get in." Jamie was excited, and her words came faster than Tony could follow, but that was just who she was. She placed his bag in the trunk, quickly arranged the others to make sure there was maximum space left over, and got into the front seat.

"Hey, Tony, how's life?" Colin asked. As always, he seemed able to summarize things down to a short, sharp sentence.

"It's good," Tony answered. He liked talking to Colin because it was never complicated or in-depth.

They pulled away from the bus stop and were on the road again. Tony sat quietly, preparing himself for the company, and the sudden change of plans. It would be fine. As long as Ricky behaved.

***

"Shit, I need to run to the store quickly," Stella said as she rummaged through her bag.

"No, you'll wait here with me. They will be here any minute," Ricky snapped, glaring at his girlfriend.

"You don't understand, I really need to go to the store. Just quickly, it's at the end of the street," she said, closing the zipper on her bag.

Ricky turned to face her, his eyes glaring. "If you've forgotten something, then you will just have to live without it. I won't have you being gone when your friends arrive. So just drop it, alright?"

Stella lowered her eyes to the ground. "Okay, sorry, you're right."

"I know. I love you." Ricky leaned over and gave Stella a quick kiss on the cheek. His lips were cold, but she didn't say anything.

The couple stood side-by-side in front on the sidewalk in front of a rundown-looking house that was owned by Ricky's mother. She was out of town, and they had enjoyed the place to themselves all weekend in anticipation of the trip. What that really meant was Ricky had spent the weekend either fucking her or complaining about having to spend time with her friends. He didn't like the idea of a cabin in the woods and certainly didn't like the idea of sharing a place with two others, especially two people that knew Stella well, and knew very little about him.

"It's going to be fine," Stella said as Ricky fidgeted.

"I know it will. They're just fucking late. If they are making me head away with them, the least they could do is be on time."

"Nobody is forcing you, babe. And besides, you're doing it with me, not them," Stella said, nervously, but fell quiet when Ricky glared across at her. "They probably went to pick up Tony first, now that I think about it."

"Tony?" Ricky's head snapped around.

"Yeah, Jamie's brother. He is coming too, I told you," Stella said

Ricky let his backpack fall to the ground. "Oh great, so the retard is coming too. That's going to be fun." Ricky's rage boiled over in an instant. His face turned a vivid shade of red, and his eyes seemed to bulge from their sockets.

It was a side of him that Stella had come to know in the past few months. As their relationship deepened, so had his controlling and jealous ways.

"He's not a retard. He's just quiet. I've known Tony for years. He's a good guy, so please don't hassle him," Stella asked as she reached to take Ricky's hand within hers.

He took it and squeezed a little too hard, causing Stella to flinch. Ricky looked at her and gave a small smile. "He better stay away from me then."

Silence fell between them, and the sounds of the street grew. A drill was rumbling somewhere inside one of the nearby homes, while three doors down an elderly man with shorts, complete with knobby knees, a tank top, and beanie hat appeared, pushing an old electric lawnmower, the bright orange cable extending back into the house like a snake. It was clear from the garden that the cable didn't quite stretch to the very end, where a six-inch strip of grass stood three times taller than the rest of the lawn.

The approaching car announced itself arrival a few moments before pulling into view. Coming down a small side street opposite as opposed to following the main road, it was clear that Colin had taken the wrong turn, but Stella breathed a sigh of relief when Ricky made no comment on the fact.

"Well sweet Jesus, they made it here after all," he cussed at the car as it swung around in a wide arc and clumsily pulled up at the curb, the passenger-side wheel mounting the sidewalk while the rear wheel on the same side was in no danger of emulating the feat.

"Hey guys, you ready to get this party started?" Colin leaned over from behind the wheel to shout through the lowered passenger-side window.

"Yeah, I am," Stella replied, a little too enthusiastically for Ricky's taste. Another glare shot in her direction from the trunk was enough to dull the excitement.

Ricky loaded his bag, throwing it haphazardly into the trunk, and stood waiting for Stella to follow suit with her own, giving a sigh of irritation when she began moving his to allow her own bags to lie flat against the carpeted base.

"You take the middle then," he growled as Stella ducked down without hesitation and slid across the seats.

"Hey Tony, it's been a while." Stella smiled at her best friend's brother.

"Hi," Tony answered, his eyes darting in Stella's direction for a fleeting moment of contact before returning to the window. It was an act born from politeness, and an attempt to make contact, rather than a rude display of disinterest.

"How have you been?" she asked, genuinely interested.

"Oh, good, good. Busy with school." Tony paused for a moment. "How about you?"

Ricky slid in beside Stella and instantly pulled her closer to him. "She's fine. Are we going to get on the road or what? We're already late," Ricky snapped.

Nobody said anything as Colin put the car into gear and pulled away from the sidewalk, while Jamie took the chance to change the playlist to something more recent. It didn't take long before she found the list she had secretly installed on Colin's phone the week before.

"Hey," Colin said, flashing her a smile.

"You didn't think you were going to listen to that all the way, do you?" Jamie leaned up and over, kissing her boyfriend on the cheek.

Colin smiled and returned his attention to the road, while in the back seat, Ricky gave a heavy sigh that showed his displeasure at the musical choice. The two girls ignored him and were soon both quietly singing along, slightly out of key and half a beat behind, but they made it work.

CHAPTER TWO

There was no real traffic on the road, and once they managed to work their way out of the city and hit I-81, it was a case of almost suspiciously open road and good times. They more than made up for the minutes lost at the start of the day and were cruising down toward Asheville with the windows down, the wind whipping through the car and music blasting through the stereo.

The playlist was more attuned to the two females in the car, but it didn't stop Colin from singing every now and then, while his fingers drummed almost constantly against the wheel. Even Tony sat with a smile on his face as the songs worked their way through his defenses and helped him relax. Only Ricky sat quietly, staring out of the window, not making any effort to talk to anybody.

Stella had tried but gave up quickly. She had already learned it was best to let Ricky be when he was in a mood. He had only hit her once, and she had started the fight, but she did not want to get into a cycle. Once was okay; she had cried, and he had apologized. It didn't even leave a bruise or anything, so it wasn't that bad, or so Stella had convinced herself.

"I'm hungry," Jamie announced not long after midday. "I skipped breakfast this morning. Can we stop off and grab a bite?"

"Why not just drive through? It's cramped in here, and I'm not hungry," Ricky said, opening his mouth for the first time.

"Well, I am, and besides, we're making good time," Jamie said, oblivious to Ricky's darker side. She didn't like him and hoped Stella didn't stay with him, but she was not afraid of him.

"You should have eaten breakfast," he replied, staring at the back of Jamie's head.

"Well, the house was all packed up. Eating wasn't an option," Jamie replied with a smile.

"I could eat," Tony added from the opposite side of the back seat, jumping to his sister's defense.

"I bet," Ricky grumbled.

"That settles it then. Burgers and a shake, coming up," Colin announced, pointing out the looming sign of a fast food restaurant in the distance.

He took the exit and they pulled away from the interstate. Despite his protestations to the contrary, Ricky still ordered a hamburger and fries when the time came.

"Let's go inside. There's more space there than in the car," Jamie said from the front seat. "It doesn't look that busy."

It was an understatement; the lot had four cars in it and no doubt at least two belonged to employees.

They pulled into a corner spot and sat for a few moments before getting out. The place was rundown, and two windows on the rear side were boarded up and covered with enough graffiti to tell them that it was not a recent act of vandalism that had necessitated the placement of the boards.

The place looked as rundown on the inside as it did on the outside. Two middle-aged women who looked about as happy to see the customers as they would be to see a proctologist walk into an examination room stood behind the double registers, while another figure stood in the kitchen. The lingering scent of stale fat and old oil hung in the air over the registers, while a layer of grease and grime over the wall-mounted menu boards made it feel as though they were reading through a haze.

The group ordered a round of cheeseburgers and fries each, but all agreed to hold off on any bathroom visits if possible.

With their food dumped onto a collection of trays, they took a seat as far away from the serving area as possible. One other couple sat in the rear corner on the opposite side. They seemed oblivious to everything going on around them, as they sat staring at one another, the tray on the table between them empty.

"You know, this isn't actually half bad," Colin said as he took a big bite, chewing enthusiastically.

"You're right. It's really good," Stella agreed as she nibbled on her burger.

They chatted as they ate, but for the most, a silence hung over them. The girls were the ones who shouldered most of the discussions, while Tony sat quietly contemplating the world, eating slowly, as was his way.

"Hurry it up, I want to get on the road," Ricky snapped after he finished wiping his mouth clean. His initial trepidation at trying the food had disappeared and he inhaled his burger and what Stella had left of hers.

Now, his impatience was shining through within moments of declaring himself ready to leave.

"No worries, Tony. Take your time, buddy," Colin said, glaring at Ricky.

Ricky said nothing but grabbed Stella's hand under the table, holding it in a strong grip that went beyond affection, through possessive and into painful territory.

"The others should arrive a few hours before us, so hopefully they can get everything set up," Jamie said as Tony finished his food and insisted on going to the bathroom.

"So how many of us are going to be there?" Ricky asked, his voice as amicable as it could possibly get.

"Seven all told. The five of us, my friend Tammy, and her friend Susan, who I think Tony will really get on with." Jamie was bubbling over with excitement, but it was hard to tell if it was the company or the chance to play matchmaker with her brother that had induced such a heightened state.

"Wonderful," Ricky said as he sat back and pulled his mobile from his pocket. "Not much of a signal in here."

Tony emerged from the bathroom looking a little worse for wear from the sights he had seen inside. Nobody asked him, and he seemed more content than usual to keep quiet.

They left, and Colin threw a cheery goodbye to the ladies behind the counter. They seemed taken aback by the gesture but managed a smile in response.

Inside the car, their bellies full and all eyes once again on the road ahead, they set off.

The traffic started to build once they neared Asheville, but the minute they turned off the interstate, it was as though they had entered a different world.

"Dude, you took the wrong exit," Ricky spoke from the back seat. He had been watching the satnav in the center console for the last hour.

"What?" Colin asked, distracting himself from the music and the road ahead.

"We were supposed to take the 26 around Johnson City," Ricky expanded, putting together his longest and politest sentence of the trip.

"Yeah, but see that red line? That's the exit we need, but it's blocked, probably an accident or something, but if we follow this road, and take a left in a few miles, it will bring us right back on track with where we need to be, just minus the delay." Colin looked in the rearview mirror, but Ricky was pressed against the door just out of view.

"Whatever. Just don't go getting us lost in some backwater mountain town," Ricky grumbled.

"I don't hear any banjos playing just yet, Ricky, so don't worry," Jamie joked from the front.

The road was bumpier than the interstate, and the older car didn't quite have the suspension of its younger years, but Colin knew what she could take.

The music had changed to classic rock four tracks previous and nobody had noticed. The heavy acoustic set filled the car and Colin tapped the wheel in time with the baseline.

For a few moments, the road they were on no longer registered on the navigation system, and it claimed they were driving through a river. When it finally came back on, the calm and collected voice told them to take the next right. Doing so felt like a bad idea, but Colin looked at the group, as best he could from the driver's seat. They decided to trust the pre-programmed machine and turned off at the first right turn they came to.

It seemed to calm the machine, who found a road in its systems and placed them on it once more.

"This doesn't feel right to me." Jamie said, looking out of the window.

They were driving through the woods now, a small two-lane road that had seen better days and was unlikely to get improved before it cracked down to the earth base.

The gloom created by the trees was almost enough to warrant headlights, but Colin held off. Instead, his mind concentrated on the road ahead. They had not seen a car in more time than they cared to admit.

"Guys, do you hear that?" Stella asked from the back seat.

"Very funny," Jamie replied, looking at her friend.

"No, I'm serious."

"Oh, shit it's my phone." Colin pulled the cell from the cupholder between him and Jamie and swiped the screen to accept the call.

"Hello?" Colin answered. "Hello?" His voice rose as he swapped hands, freeing up his right to find the volume controls on the stereo.

"Colin, look out!" Stella screamed, thrusting her arm forward. Jamie snapped her head to the front and saw the small figure as it ran before their car, coming to a stop in the center of the lane.

Colin yelled and twisted the wheel, as everybody in the car cried out as they were thrown hard to the left. The tires screeched, and the car spun, its rear-end not slowing down to match the front. For a few hair-raising moments, it felt as if they were going to roll, but as the car finished its rotation, everything leveled out.

They came to a stop in the same lane but facing back down the way they had come.

"What was that?" Colin asked, his voice raspy as he gasped for air.

"It looked like a kid," Jamie answered.

"I don't see it," Stella offered.

"Did I hit it?" Colin asked, panic filling his voice.

"No," Ricky offered.

"Maybe he ran away," Tony piped up, the near miss enough to bring him out of his shell, at least long enough to speak.

"Jesus Christ," Colin said, undoing his belt and reaching for the door.

He paused when Jamie placed a hand on his leg.

"You don't need to go out. Maybe we just imagined it. I mean, there's nobody out there." Colin nodded, heeding the tone of her voice. The last thing he wanted was to scare her, or any of the others any more than they now were.

He remembered the phone. He had dropped it when grabbing at the wheel. He found it in the footwell, partially lodged under the accelerator. The call had disconnected and while there was a fresh crack in the screen, it was still in good working order. Colin was surprised how much his hand trembled as he worked his way through entering a password and into the list of recent called.

"It was Tammy," he said, staring at the number, taking a few seconds to let the recognition come to him.

"Call her back," Jamie urged. Her normally pale cheeks were flushed from the shock of everything that had happened.

The phone rang a few times before it was answered.

"Hey, Tammy, Tammy?" Colin pressed the button for speakerphone so the others could hear it too.

"Tammy, it's Jamie, where are you guys?" There was still no answer, but a strange raspy sound came through the speakers. It was followed by something that sounded like footsteps.

A scream erupted from the phone before it suddenly went dead.

"Tammy!" Jamie cried out as if she could somehow pull her friend through the phone.

"Oh my God, what happened? You heard that, right?" Jamie babbled in the front seat, her words spewing fast from her mouth, but only half the speed with which more were forming in her brain.

"Maybe it was nothing," Stella offered, leaning forward to put a hand on Jamie's shoulder.

"Perhaps it was a bad connection, like the lines got crossed or something," Tony whispered to his sister.

"Yeah or a pocket dial," Stella offered. "I've lost count of the number of people I have called with my butt."

Tony turned to look at Stella, and she smiled back at him. He shifted his position in the back seat and fell quiet once more.

"Well, let's get moving before some hillbilly clan comes to snatch us too," Ricky unhelpfully offered.

"You don't think...?" Jamie couldn't even bring herself to say it.

"Dude, chill with the asshole attitude," Colin spat, his words hard. They sounded foreign coming from his mouth.

"Fuck you and drive," Ricky snarled.

Tony watched as Stella reached out and placed a hand on Ricky's leg. His came down on hers, the grip strong because his knuckles bulged and his hand seemed to tremor with pent rage. Stella said nothing but had to pull her hand back again.

"You don't have to be such a dick all the time," Colin replied as he put the car into gear. His dislike for Ricky was clear.

The atmosphere in the car changed, and while Colin tried to get the music going again, Jamie reached right out and lowered it down to nothing but a gentle background noise. She didn't speak, but sat on the seat, staring out at the trees. Her eyes brimmed with tears, and she chewed her bottom lip but managed to keep her composure.

"They'll be fine. I'm sure it's nothing," Colin said, taking her hand in his before raising it to his mouth to plant a kiss on her fingers.

"Will you pull over for a second?" Jamie asked, unbuckling her belt before giving Colin a chance to ask why.

"Sure."

The car stopped on the side of the road and Jamie opened the door. Colin followed suit, jumping out to meet her by the trunk.

"You okay?" he asked, putting his arms around her shoulder.

"Yeah, it's just I want to drive for a bit, if that's okay." She looked at him and batted her eyelids.

"Sure, yeah." Colin gave her the keys and kiss on the cheek. "It might give Ricky a heart attack too."

"He's a jerk, but Stella's my best friend."

"He's more than a jerk," Colin added, before walking around and getting into the passenger seat.

To his credit, Ricky said nothing at the change of roles up front but gave a groan when the pop songs returned to the radio.

"Driver picks the music." Jamie smiled at Colin, who said nothing and smiled in return.

The satnav continued to be their guide, yet worryingly, the roads continued to get smaller and smaller, yet the longer they drove, the more people seemed to relax, and the memory of the phone call and the spin became just that: Memories. In the back seat, Ricky fell into an awkward sleep, snoring with his face pressed against the car window, while Stella tried to get chatting to Tony. Jamie watched them through the rearview mirror.

Tony didn't have many friends, and as far as she knew, he had never had a girlfriend. She felt bad for him at times, but he always assured her he was happy. He was tall, strong, and had the same green eyes as her, inherited from their mother.

"So how is it at school? Better than you expected?" Stella asked, keeping the conversation light.

"Yes, it's hard at times, but the courses are fun." Tony turned and looked at Stella briefly.

"Good, I'm glad. Do you get much free time?" she asked with genuine interest.

"Oh yes, quite a bit. But I have a job too. I work in a bookstore; well, it's more of a coffee house now, but they sell books too. Do you like to read?" Tony asked, bringing the topic 'round to something less personal, but equally telling about a person.

"Yes, I mean, I've not read much this last year, and its normally cheesy chick books, but I like to read." Stella smiled, her deep hazel eyes and her tanned skin giving her a near exotic complexion.

"Books are a great way to escape, I always find. I don't socialize much, but with a book, well, I always have somewhere to go. Do you read fantasy novels at all?" Tony's expression changed, and his enjoyment of the interaction made Stella smile.

"Yes," she lied.

"Oh, then you should check out M Matthias. He's an indie author but writing some really great stuff." Tony smiled from ear to ear.

Stella found herself smiling as a result. "Thanks, I'll keep my eyes open for him."

Their conversation continued, moving through books and onto movies. Tony spoke easy and without burden to Stella, and she responded equally, chatting in a way she had not done for quite some time.

"Are you sure this is taking us back to the interstate?" Stella leaned forward to ask Jamie, as they took another advised turn and found themselves passing the first of several run-down shacks that clearly had people living in them. Lines of washing and smoke from fires and smokehouses proved that.

"I'm just following this thing, but I think she's even more lost than I would be." Jamie pointed at the navigation system. The map no longer showed any roads and had them driving across a field of white.

"Yeah, I'm thinking I should have installed the update before we left," Colin said as he picked up the unit and started pressing buttons.

"Well, maybe there's a town or something up here. We can stop and ask for directions," Stella offered as she watched out of the window as two kids ran from one of the shacks.

They were chasing one another, their faces pulled back into smiles of innocence and delight. "It's so sad that people have to live like that." Stella sank back into her seat and folded her arms across her chest.

"It's also nice that people can live like that and still find the positive, and smile," Tony added. "I think, sometimes, we get too caught up in what we want, we don't think about what we already have." Tony looked at Stella, and caught his sister looking at him via the rear-view mirror, a smile spread across her lips.

Tony wasn't sure why, but he smiled back.

"That's exactly it, Tony," Colin piped up and turned around in the passenger seat. "We are all too concerned with having the biggest or the best of something."

"Maybe, but I still feel sorry for them," Stella added.

"Sorry for who? These hillbillies?" Ricky spoke, his voice groggy with sleep. "If they want a better life, they should just go earn it like the rest of us."

Ricky's arrival killed the conversation, and Stella sat back, rigid in the seat, her hands folded in her lap.

Tony studied her for a few moments before he looked up to see Ricky staring at him. The man's jaw was clenched ,and his eyes seemed to darken as they bored a hole into Tony's chest. To his credit, Ricky said nothing, but it took Stella's hand on his leg to get him to sit back.

"Well, it looks like there's a town or something up ahead," Jamie spoke, pointing at a sign tied to a tree by the side of the road. The metal supports had long since disappeared.

The name was hard to read, as green slime covered most of the letters, and those that were visible had faded away, but it didn't matter. They had no plans on staying.

"Let's pull over at a store. We can ask directions, and I need to grab something anyway," Stella said to Jamie, laying a hand on her shoulder as she spoke.

"This again. I told you, you don't need anything," Ricky growled, clearly louder than he intended.

"If she wants something, she can buy something," Tony muttered.

"Who asked you? We're already lost in the middle of fucking nowhere. Now really isn't the time to go shopping." Ricky glared at Tony but caught himself and settled back down when he saw the way Colin had turned to stare at him.

While he was a gentle man, Colin stood over six foot three and worked out regularly, giving him a solid appearance, even if he hid his true physique behind baggy shirts and an easy-going attitude.

The town was hidden away and clearly did not get much passing traffic. The buildings were, at best, in need of renovation, and at worst, held together by nothing more than spit and hope. The road was paved but had likely never seen any maintenance. Houses lined the street, with several side roads branching off at regular intervals. The side roads were unpaved, nothing more than dirt tracks. The cars were mostly pick-up trucks or rust buckets that would probably fall apart if anybody tried to drive them further than from one end of the town to another.

A few people were milling about; an old woman was sitting on a chair outside what looked to be a church, her tiny body making the chair look comically large. A group of children stood frozen, watching the car as if it were some unbeknown source of wonder or possible witchcraft. Their eyes followed the vehicle as it went along, and only once it was past did they return to their games.

"We are definitely not on the right track," Jamie said as she slowed the car to a crawl as she went over a pothole in the road.

"Let's just get out of here. Why don't we turn around and head back to the interstate? I'd rather sit in traffic than be stuck out here," Jamie offered to the group.

"I reckon we are only an hour or so away, two tops. Turning back now is going to more than double that," Colin said, laying out the facts.

"You want to keep driving through places like this?" Jamie asked, pointing to a modified tractor that drove past them. Six people were situated on or around the seat, with two merely holding onto the roll-bars that had been crudely welded onto the tractor's frame.

"What the fuck is that?" Colin mused, staring at the contraption and the people on it.

"It's probably what passed for normal around here. I'm with Jamie," Ricky said as he watched a man with a beard that hid close to his entire face turn into a side road, a bottle of liquor in one hand, and his cock in the other.

Jamie slowed the car as they pulled up to a red light. The tractor stood idling, the hoots and hollers of its occupants falling quiet as all eyes turned toward their car.

The group was all male, and their eyes instantly found Jamie behind the wheel. The slow smiles that appeared on their faces were nothing short of lecherous.

"We can turn around up here." Jamie pointed ahead to a grocery store parking lot. Four pick-ups stood guard outside the building, which looked almost derelict. Had it not been for the neon sign proclaiming that the shop was open, they would have assumed it to be just that.

"Can we please stop? I really need to run in and grab something. I'll be two seconds." Stella stared at Jamie, who looked at her through the rear-view mirror.

Jamie nodded and pulled away from the lights, the tractor beside them roaring like the king of the jungle as it pulled away and sped down the road, the heavy stench of burning fuel lingering in the air like the cheap perfume of a dangerous woman.

They pulled off the road and into the parking lot. Jamie brought the car as close to the door as she could, avoiding parking directly beside the two large trucks that stood on either side of the door, like bouncers.

"Do you want me to go with you?" Jamie asked, her hand hovering over the key.

Stella looked at her friend but shook her head. "I'll be fine. It's just one thing I need."

Turning, Stella looked at Ricky, who glared at her with a look of annoyance, and made no attempt to get out of the car to let her through. So with an angry sigh, she twisted towards Tony, who took the hint immediately and started to unbuckle himself.

"No need, Tony," Stella said, reaching over to open the door before lifting her leg and stepping over his lap. "I got this."

She paused for a moment, straddling him, her chest pressed close to him so that he couldn't help but look down the front of her loose-fitting top. She let out a slow breath, and the air around Tony filled with a combination of her floral perfume and the minty freshness of her toothpaste. With a quick and effortless ease, she stepped out of the car and dragged her left leg across Tony's lap. She pushed the door closed as she walked away, leaving Tony in the back seat, locked in Ricky's glare.

Tony watched Stella walk away, but as he turned back from the window, he saw Ricky staring him down. He didn't blink, and the muscles in his neck bulged as he clenched his jaw, rage bubbling from him with such force it could almost be felt as a wave of heat.

Averting his gaze, Tony found himself watching Stella disappear into the store. He swallowed hard and tried to ignore the growing silence.

Up front, Colin sat playing with the satnav unit. "I just can't get it to pick up where we are." He replaced the unit in the holder. According to technology, they were parked in the woods some distance from the road.

"Leave it," Jamie said. "We'll be on our way soon and then it will pick us up again."

CHAPTER THREE

Stella had never felt angrier as she strode away from the car. Her relationship with Ricky was rocky at best, but she had hoped a trip into the woods would give him to chance to relax and show her the funny and charming guy he had been when they first met. Now, her blood boiled beneath her skin and she clenched her fists with such force her nails threatened to cut into the palm of her hands.

She refused to look back as she marched toward the store, even though she could feel his eyes watching her walk away.

She hoped Ricky would behave. She knew he saw how she stepped across Tony to get out of the car. She paused with her hand on the door handle. She had known Tony forever. He had always been shy and quiet, but all of a sudden, there was something about him, about his presence. Maybe it was just her getting older and learning how complicated relationships were. She shook her head as if hoping to dislodge the thoughts that were forming there.

Pulling the door open, she walked inside. The shop smelled old, like dust and stale water. The door creaked as it swung closed behind her, and Stella was swept away by the sensation of being locked in.

The register stood to her left, whoever sat behind it hidden by the hunting magazine they were reading. The lighting was dim at best, the long fluorescent lights covered by plastic housing that seemed to be coated in a layer of grime that significantly reduced their efficiency. She could hear a strong buzzing sound that seemed to follow around her as she walked inside. It was hot and stuffy, which only added to the uncomfortable atmosphere.

Eager to get in and out as soon as possible, Stella hurried down the central aisle. The shelves were bent and crooked, with sections that stood empty and stained, like bruises still lingering after years of abuse. A cooling unit ran along the back of the store. The lights only worked in three of the four units, but the contents were unmistakable. Beer, ice cold, and screaming to be drunk. Stella thought about buying a six-pack for them but changed her mind when she saw the man standing by the central unit.

A towering man stood with a bulging gut stretching the confines of his greasy T-shirt, which billowed over the top of his overall trousers like a balloon when squeezed through the middle.

Stella stopped in her tracks and spun around. The man paid her no mind, his attention seemingly held by the beer before him.

As she hurried down another aisle, her mind began to wonder if they would even stock what she needed, when suddenly, it was there. Two choices, and only one box of each left. Neither was the brand she normally bought and so Stella paused to take a look, picking up both boxes to read the labels.

She didn't hear the man walk behind her, but she heard his slow intake of breath and the sticky wet sound of his tongue wetting his lips.

"I knew you smelled good." The sneering voice had a slimy tone to it, as if the grease that covered the man's clothes had also seeped through to his insides, drowning with words as they were born in his throat.

Stella spun around, more an automatic reaction than any conscious decision. The fat man was standing so close, his belly was almost pressing against her. His scent was heavy and unavoidable: the stench of motor oil and grease, mixed with body odor and the sour scent of unwashed teeth.

"Excuse me?" Stella asked, her voice trembling. She had to crane her neck to look the man in the eyes, to see anything other than his belly. She wanted to take a step back but couldn't, the shelving blocking her way.

The man looked at her for a while. A heavy mustache hid his lips but could do nothing to shield her from the sight of his tongue darting from his mouth, like a snake tasting the air. "You smell good like a woman should smell. That's good, that's really good."

The words cause Stella to break out in goosebumps over her entire body while the shudder that ran through her caused a visible reaction that she could not hide from him. He laughed but made no attempt to move.

"Stella?" a voice called from the far end of the aisle.

"Everything alright?" another voice joined in.

Turning her head, Stella saw Jamie and Tony standing side by side, as if they were guards blocking the fat man's escape route.

"Ain't no problem here," the fat man said as he finally stepped away and strode toward the front of the store, a couple of six-packs in his meaty hands.

Rather than going around them, the man pushed through the middle of Jamie and Tony, looking at Jamie as he walked through, but the moment he broke their line, his eyes turned to Tony.

Stella watched him walk away and found herself shaking by the time her friends reached her.

"Are you okay? What happened?" Jamie asked, wrapping her arm around her friend. "You're shaking."

"Nothing, nothing, he just surprised me, that's all. Let's just get out of here." Stella stood up and forced herself to calm down. Yet she didn't move until the fat man had finished paying for his beer.

He stopped by the door and looked from the man behind the register over to the three of them as a greasy smirk passed over his face. It was a quick movement, like a shadow altering the impression he gave before it passed on, revealing the lecherous scowl that appeared to be his version of a resting bitch face.

Stella turned back to the items she had replaced on the shelf and moved to grab them again. She froze and looked around, still shaken by her encounter with the brute. She reached again, picking them up, and with a quick look at the suddenly inquisitive eyes of the man behind the register, she replaced them again.

The man behind the register smiled; his eyes had the same leering quality as his greasy friend.

"Do you really need them?" Tony asked, his voice a whisper.

"Well, yeah," Stella answered, looking at him as if to ask why else she would stop to buy them.

"Come on then, I'll pay for them." Tony reached out and collected the two boxes and walked to the register.

The man waiting to serve them seemed almost disappointed when Tony approached him, holding a box of tampons in each hand.

He put them on the countertop and stared at the man. Stella and Jamie stood a step back, waiting for something to happen.

The man looked past Tony and stared straight at Stella. He smiled, and his eyes glinted with malicious intent.

"Nothing to be ashamed of, darling, it's all natural," he said as he picked up the box and started reading the labels. "Natural and healthy, just like the rest of you, I bet."

"Can we just pay for it?" Tony said, his voice shaking as he stepped outside of his comfort zone, confronting the man behind the counter.

"Steady on, son, I don't mean nothing by it. Just saying, good-looking girls like you shouldn't be embarrassed by Mother Nature. If your fella here is a real man, he'd not care and go in any way." The man returned his gaze to Tony and smiled, testing him, probing for a reaction.

Tony lowered his eyes, the pressure of the confrontation too much for him. The man started to laugh. A slow snort at first, as if he were actively trying to restrain himself, but when that became too much effort, he dropped the pretense.

"So we got three pussies here then. Tell me, is one box for you, son?" The man burst out laughing again, slapping his hands against his thighs before he doubled over to try and catch his breath.

When he stood up again, his eyes were red with tears, and his mouth hung open as he took gulping breaths. He only had a few teeth remaining in his mouth and they were yellow and broken, and for a moment, as he stood with his jaw agape, he looked every inch as insane as he sounded.

Seeing her brother struggle, Jamie stepped forward and pulled a note from Tony's wallet. She slapped it down on the counter and turned to storm away.

"Come on now, I'm just fuckin' with you." The man wheezed as he wiped a trail of snot from under his nose with the back of his hand. He inspected the result before smearing it on his trousers. "Not often we get new folk passing through. Although, you're the second group we had come in today mind you. The first couple of gals were game for a laugh though."

There was something in the man's voice that put them on edge, but Jamie turned back to him nonetheless.

"Others?" she asked, not moving from her spot by the door, disinterested in getting any closer to the man, regardless of what he had to say.

"Yeah, two young girls. Ripe things too." He licked his lips and paused for a moment as if savoring the memory of their presence.

Jamie looked at the others, and she could see from their expressions they were thinking the same as her: The phone call, just before they almost totaled the car; the muffled sounds and the scream.

Jamie felt her heart rate quicken as she stared at the man, her unease growing into fear.

"What were their names?" Her voice had a strong quiver to it.

"Well, now I don't think I asked 'em that particular question. They came in looking for directions, said they were heading to a cabin for the weekend." The man paused to snort back the next line of snot that had planned to make an escape through his nose. "I told 'em the way to go, and that was that."

Jamie took a step closer, shrugging off Tony's hand as he reached for her shoulder. "Well, what did they look like?" She stopped short of the counter, her words not so much a question but rather more an accusation. It was as if she were trying to get him to stumble, to trap him in a lie.

The man stood up from the stool, his body heavily slanted to one side. His back gave an audible pop as he rose, then with a grimace, he leaned forward on the counter, lowering himself until he rested on his elbows.

"Well, they were about your height. One had blonde hair and tits bigger than yours, wore this perfume that got you damned drunk it smelled so sweet on her. You could just about imagine how good the rest of her smelled. The other was a bit bigger. Some good meat on her bones. Not fat, mind you, just got enough cushion on her frame and an ass that was better than yours too." He looked Jamie up and down before giving a disapproving shake of his head.

"Where did they go?" she asked, almost pleading.

"Told you, I gave 'em directions and sent 'em on their way." The man raised his arm and pointed with a gnarled hand towards the road out of town.

Jamie turned back to her brother and Stella. Her friend had pushed close to Tony, and still looked shaken by everything that had happened. She gripped the boxes of tampons hard enough to crush the packaging.

"That's them," she said in a near whisper as if admitting it would somehow spell the end for all of them. She turned back to the counter, where the man had once again taken a seat. "Can you give us the same directions?"

The man was still for a moment and then smiled, his long front tooth emerging from between his lips like the descending fang of a geriatric vampire. "Sure, I don't see why not. You say you're friends and all that. I told them to head out of town and take a left just after the old farmhouse. You'll know it when you see it because there's only one. Now, it's not the best quality road, but it'll take you around the blockage and bring you up to the cabin in not too much time. Yep, that'll do it. One turn and then a few straight roads."

"Thank you," Jamie offered, her words still tentative. She went as far as to back away from the counter until she reached her brother and Stella. Together, they turned and left, hurrying back to the car.

"You've got to be fucking kidding me," Ricky growled as he saw what Stella was holding as she climbed back into the car.

"What?" she asked, embarrassed even further by the way he grabbed one of the boxes and held it up for all to see.

"This. I mean, come on." His annoyance grew, and within moments, the fear from the store was replaced by the awkward silence that seemed to follow Stella's boyfriend everywhere he went.

"You can't fight nature, but don't worry. It'll be cool. We'll party a little. This weekend is all about relaxing and getting ready for college," Stella said, snatching back the tampons.

"This place looks like it's found a way to fight nature pretty well," Colin said from the front passenger seat, as a means of breaking the silence.

Jamie laughed first, and then Stella. Ricky soon followed in a rare moment of calm. Caught off guard by the comment, he couldn't help but roll with it.

"See, you don't want me turning into a hillbilly, do you?" Stella asked, pouting.

Ricky looked at her, and then out of the window, his intention to ignore the question, but his eyes fell on a group of kids, running and playing on a muddy front lawn of a dilapidated house that looked to be sinking on one side, the slant of its frame so pronounced. The children, three boys and one girl, all looked as if they had some affliction or some other genetic malfunction, for their faces were too crooked while their eyes and mouths didn't fit the rest of them.

Ricky shuddered and turned back to Stella. "I'll keep you as you are, thanks." There was little else he could say given the circumstances.

They drove on through the town, following the main road, eager to see how soon it led them out and back onto the open road. They drove past a garage where the fat man from the store was sitting, drinking one of the beers. He looked at them and raised his can in recognition of the stares. Behind him, a car sat under a grease-covered sheet. There were no other signs of work in progress, so they reasoned he had stopped for the day.

"Would you look at that guy," Ricky said.

"I'd rather not," Stella said, shrinking back into her seat, hyper-aware of both men sitting on either side of her.

They drove in silence, none of them in the mood for music. The road out of town took them along a series of ever-weaker-looking homes, and while the state of the road kept them from moving too fast, they were all eager to leave the place behind them.

"I guess that's it." Jamie pointed at the abandoned farmhouse that loomed on the horizon.

The large two-and-a-half story building stared at them, blank windows an empty gaze, watching the world go by. The previously white-washed wooden panels had long since faded, and the remaining paint had started to peel away in thick strips. A leafless vine had started to climb up the sides of the house, its spreading limbs reaching up to the crumbling eaves on either end. Their reddish, purple color looked like an infection spread through what remained of a once-glorious building, and the first signs of its continued spread against the front-facing side of the building was nothing but a confirmation of the terminal state the structure was in.

"So, what did that old dude say? We turn left?" Colin asked, looking at the turning ahead of them. Jamie had slowed the car to a crawl, hesitant to make the wrong decision.

"Yep," Jamie said, swallowing hard. Her hands fiercely gripped the wheel.

"I think we should go straight. Fuck what they said," Ricky offered from the back seat.

"You did hear the scream on the phone. What if they set a trap for the others?" Stella offered.

"Did you see these people? That level of planning would be beyond them," Ricky said, sneering.

"Come on, dude, lay off them a little," Colin said from the front seat.

Ricky stiffened immediately but held his temper in check. "Whatever. Go left, go straight, turn fucking right if you want; just get us there so I can have a damned drink."

"Trust me, we all want one with you in the car," Colin replied, turning to throw his own glare at the already flammable Ricky.

Stella shifted in her seat, subconsciously moving closer to Tony. She had had reservations about going on the trip, having seen Ricky's temper in action, but Jamie had convinced her, yet now they had not even arrived and Ricky had pissed them all off.

"Fuck you. Just get us there and stay out of my way this weekend," Ricky growled, his hands clenched into fists in his lap.

"My thoughts exactly," Colin replied, his words and demeanor cool and calm.

Jamie pressed hard on the gas, the sudden lurch of the car shutting everybody up, and she drove on past the farmhouse, continuing on the paved road. She shuddered as she drove by the abandoned building as if she could feel the air around it being poisoned with the same sickness that caused it to be left behind to rot.

A long bend brought them to a quick stop when they saw the trees that had indeed fallen across the road. Two of them had been felled, each from woods on either side of the paving; not quite opposite each other, but close enough for the difference to be ignored.

"Well, I'll be damned," Colin said, "the old bugger was right."

"Isn't that convenient?" Ricky said in a mocking tone.

"What do you mean?" Jamie asked, not taking her eyes off the trees.

Ricky chuckled before answering. "This redneck just happens to know of some trees that happen to have fallen when we need to pass through town. I'm telling you, we turn around and go their way, they'll be waiting to ass-fuck the lot of us all night long."

"Ew, gross," Stella said, giving Ricky a shove.

"What, I've seen Deliverance, I know how these things work." Ricky stared at the trees. "Whatever happens, we end up squealing like stuck pigs, and those inbreds will be braying like wild horses."

"Shut up," Jamie said as she put the car into reverse. "We'll take that side road, and I promise I won't stop to pick up any hitchhikers."

Ricky sat back in his seat and said nothing as Jamie swung the car around in a tight turn and headed back toward the farmhouse. The sun had started to set, disappearing quickly behind the hills, the orange glow that marked the incineration of another day painting the house in a fierce glow that made it look even more sinister than on first viewing.

Turning right, they drove on, the silence between them still awkward, but quashed by the tension of the unknown that seemingly lay both before and behind them.

It was near dark by the time they pulled up outside a cabin. They had not come across another car the entire drive. Their run-in with the tractor back in the town had been the last time they came close to another vehicle.

"Is this really it?" Colin asked, unable to hide his disappointment.

The cabin was small and looked as if it was in need of some repairs. A light burned on the inside, however, and it was the only one they had seen since turning off the main road. The distance matched what they had estimated also, but something still didn't sit right with the group.

"I guess," Jamie said.

"I don't see any other cars," Stella offered, expecting to see Jamie's friends at least coming out to greet them.

There was nothing. The woods seemed closer, as if the darkness was somehow compressing everything, the shadows not just beating back the light, but the very space that it occupied; a second world that existed only under the guise of the night.

"This has to be it. I mean, we've been traveling the right amount of time, and well, the GPS is on the fritz but it matches with the distance, look." Jamie pointed at the unit which proudly announced that their destination had been reached.

"Have any of you been here before?" Ricky asked, looking at the cabin in disbelief.

"No, it was Tammy's place; well, her family's. But, come on, look, a light is on, and the satnav says we are here. We're just spooked because of that weird guy in the store. Tammy probably went for a walk, or drove into town again to get some food," Jamie reasoned.

"Really? Walked or drove somewhere? Why didn't we see them?" Ricky asked, patience wearing thin.

"Hey, will you cut it out? We've all had a long day. Let it go, and let's take a look inside. It's getting colder out, and I fancy the idea of a softer seat than this and a cold beer," Colin offered, addressing the group even though his eyes bored straight into Ricky.

"Fine." Ricky opened the car door and got out, slamming it shut behind him.

"That's quite a catch you've got there," Colin said before getting out of the car along with Jamie.

Stella lowered her head and let out a long breath. "I don't like him, but as long as he is good to you, then other opinions don't matter," Tony spoke softly before opening the door.

Getting out, he held it open for Stella, who looked up at him with tear-filled eyes and pain etched into every inch of her features.

Colin knocked on the cabin's front door, but there was no answer. He tried the handle, first pulling and then pushing. It was a little stiff, the door swollen slightly too large for the frame, but with a little shoulder power, it opened. The warmth welcomed them in with open arms, and that fact alone was enough to put them a little more at ease.

CHAPTER FOUR

The cabin was smaller than they had imagined yet had a well-kept and homely feel to it. A table with space for four, two sofas, and a television hung on the wall. A strangely patterned rug was painful on the eyes but at least offered something other than a wood finish. It was also largely hidden by a coffee table, which made it more bearable.

Colin and Tony left the others to find their bearings while they went and got the bags out of the car. They had asked if Ricky wanted to help, but he just shook his head and went to the fridge to look for a beer.

When they returned, having managed to bring all of the bags in one trip, Ricky had found what he sought and was parked on the sofa, flicking through the TV channels, trying to find something that showed anything but static.

"This has got to be the right place," Jamie said as she skipped up to Colin, handed him a cold beer, and kissed him deeply. "The fridge is full of beer and I found a few bottles of liquor too. Tammy's parents keep this place well-stocked."

They kissed again, and Colin twisted the top off his beer and wrapped his other arm around Jamie. "It looks like a nice place." He nodded as he spoke. The whole day had not gone as planned, but now that they were there, everything seemed less of an issue, already fading to the category of an amusing anecdote in the annals of their history.

"TV is dead," Ricky said, as he downed the rest of his beer and walked to get another one.

"That's cool, we'll just chat and chill until the others arrive," Jamie said as her hand worked its way under Colin's shirt.

"Where do you think they are anyway?" Tony asked, walking over to the main window in the living room. He closed the curtains but only after staring out into the dark for a moment.

"I think they either got lost or got caught in the traffic we avoided," Colin said, pulling his lips away from Jamie's neck. "They probably called to say they were staying in a motel or something and will hook up with us tomorrow."

Stella stood alone until Tony moved next to her. "Well, what about all the drinks?" she asked, circling her finger to point that each of them was holding a cold beer.

"Maybe they keep it stocked. I don't know," Colin offered. It was a weak answer, but they were all eager to accept it so that they could get on with the trip

The group settled onto the sofas, which could seat five in a pinch. Jamie and Colin took one and were soon cuddled up together, lost in their closeness and blissfully oblivious to the others around them, while Stella eventually moved next to Ricky. "Come sit, Tony." She patted the space beside her.

Tony played with his beer for a second, twisting the bottle in his hands. It was still his first, unlike the others who had all downed one cold bottle before closing the fridge.

The sofa was unsuspectingly soft, and Tony leaned back into the seating. After being stuck in the car for so long, it was a relief to be sitting on something so comfortable. Even if he was opposite his sister and her amorous boyfriend, and next to the girl he had had a crush on for longer than he cared to remember, and her idiot boyfriend.

Tony had only ever met Ricky twice before, and he hadn't liked him on either of those occasions. Given the way he had behaved during their journey had been nothing but confirmation for Tony. Ricky was not a good guy.

"It's peaceful out here," he said, his voice soft, almost timid sounding.

"What was that?" Stella asked, turning toward him. Her lips glistened from the beer she had swallowed.

"Nothing important. Just that it's peaceful out here. In the woods, in nature." Tony felt his cheeks blush.

"I didn't realize you were a big outdoorsman," Stella replied.

"I'm not. Not really. I just appreciate the quiet when I find it," Tony replied.

"The very poetic." Stella smiled and put a hand on Tony's leg. "Don't you think the peace and quiet is nice, babe?"

Ricky had just finished his third beer and was playing with the empty bottle. "What?" he asked.

"I said the peace and quiet is nice, isn't it." Stella removed her hand from Tony's knee and turned to look at her boyfriend. "What's up? You're all sulky."

Ricky said nothing for a moment, chewing his cheek as he continued to stare at the bottle in his hands. "Let's go to bed," he finally spoke.

"Excuse me?" Stella asked.

"I said let's go to bed. It's quiet, but I want to make some noise, besides. Those two are putting on a free show for everybody anyway." He pointed at the loved-up couple on the opposite sofa with the neck of his bottle.

"Well, I get it, but I told you, I'm … well, you know." Stella lowered her voice, and Tony turned his head to the other side of the room out of politeness.

"Yeah, well, there are other solutions to that problem too, you know." Ricky grabbed Stella's hand and got up.

"Hey, I said no." She pulled her hand back and fell back into the sofa, against Tony, who had turned his head just in time to brace for Stella collapsing against him.

The commotion was enough to break up the lovebirds on the other sofa. Colin sprang to his feet, grabbing out at Ricky, while Jamie jumped toward her friend.

The sudden change shook Tony, who jumped up from the seat, unsure how to respond. Jamie had her arm around Stella, while Colin and Ricky had hold of each other's shirts like a pair of hockey players preparing to throw down.

"Guys, quit it," Tony said, moving to separate the pair.

He moved towards them, but only made it three paces before something hard and heavy crashed against the outside of the cabin.

The impact shook the whole building and brought them all to their feet, heads snapping away from the conflict and toward the front door.

"What was that?" Stella asked, her voice a whisper.

"It was probably nothing," Tony said, stepping forward closer to the door.

"That was not nothing," Stella said, catching Tony by the arm to stop him from wandering too far away.

"Well, maybe it was your friends. I saw genius over there lock the door once we all got inside," Ricky said, nodding towards Colin. "They probably wanted to charge in and found themselves meeting solid wood."

"Then you go open it and see," Colin growled in return.

"They're not my friends," Ricky was quick to reply.

The pair stood square to one another again when the door began to rattle in the frame. The rattle became a violent shake which was followed by a series of thudding blows dealt to the cabin's outer wall.

The crash of something hitting the wood echoed around the living room. It sounded as though they were surrounded. It was as if the cabin was being pelted by hailstones the size of tennis balls. The wooden boards creaked and wailed, the abuse so bad it warranted the agonized cries, if not as a mere testament to the brute force of what was being reigned down upon them.

The girls screamed and clung to each other, collapsing onto the sofa in terror. Colin turned to them, looking around frantically for some way to protect them. Likewise, Tony sat beside them, leaning forward as if making to offer himself up before whatever was out there came after them.

The onslaught escalated to the point that Tony was sure the cabin was going to collapse when as suddenly as it started, it ended. There was no final crash or heavy thud to mark the occasion, but rather the high-toned ping of glass cracking, a silver trail that marched a jagged pattern from left to right across the main living room window, splintering at several points, offering hesitant diversions.

"You still think it was their friends?" Colin asked, all the anger swept away from his voice.

Ricky didn't offer any answer. He had backed away from the group, stepping deeper into the room toward the kitchen area.

"Is it gone?" Stella asked from the sofa.

"I think so," Tony said, sitting down beside her.

As he sat, Jamie rose and threw herself into Colin's arms, searching for comfort and protection. For a while, nobody moved or dared even speak.

The cabin creaked and groaned, like an old fighter standing up to face the final round. The sound of the night suddenly seemed to seep through the wood and sent the temperature inside plummeting.

"Someone should really go outside and check," Ricky said from behind the others.

"Go ahead," Colin answered, not taking his arm away from Jamie or his eyes away from the door.

"It was probably just a deer or something?" Ricky said, backtracking.

"A deer," Jamie agreed, her voice robotic, the words spoken as if she was held in a trance.

"Yeah, it got lost, running from something, and collided with the cabin," Colin said, trying to validate the theory.

"Or maybe raccoons," Jamie said, still zoned out.

"Or both, raccoons chasing a deer," Colin said, his grip tightening around Jamie's shoulders, as he pulled her closer and closer to him.

Tony sat with Stella beside him, his heart pounding in his chest. He looked at the others with his eyes only, his head locked into position as if his neck had been fused into one solid stump of bone. His chest felt light and his body tingled as if he stood on the cusp of a case of whole-body pins and needles.

He listened, straining his ears to hear something, anything. He had always been told he had great hearing, but try as he might, all he could hear was his heart hammering in his ears and the sobs coming from beside him.

Suddenly aware of the closeness of another person, he looked at Stella. She had her face in her hands and was trembling with heavy, visible shudders. Instinctively, Tony reached out and put his arm around her. He was surprised to find that she offered no resistance and seemed to collapse against him, melting into his embrace.

Looking up, Tony saw Ricky's gaze locked on him. What he saw in his eyes was an anger beyond rage, but also, buried within it, a sense of relief. Tony reasoned it was because it meant he didn't have to worry about Stella and her tears.

"It's going to be alright," Tony whispered. "I'll go check."

He stood up and Stella sank back into the sofa, the worst of her fear abated. She sat staring forward and only reacted once Tony had collected the fire iron from beside the large open fire and started walking towards the door.

In fact, his movements had gone unnoticed by them all. Their own fear and racing minds held them prisoners until it was too late to stop Tony from doing what he had planned.

Walking across the cabin, the fire iron a heavy yet comforting weight in his hands, Tony reached the door, twisted the simple lock, and pushed it open.

"Tony, stop!" he heard Jamie call, but her words were soft, so as not to bring whatever had been out there back again. Thus, the power and force of her command were muted and held no impact on Tony or his decision.

It was a full dark out, the light fading fast once the sun disappeared behind the hills. With no sign of external lighting, it looked as if the cabin had been picked up and dropped into a void, much like Dorothy, only they took the wrong exit on the way to Oz and were now stuck, stranded in the wastelands.

Tony forced his breathing to slow down, and listened. He heard nothing, not even the sounds of the night, which he had expected to be close to deafening with them being so far away from any major population.

He stepped forward, crossing the threshold, but not leaving the doorway completely.

"Tony, get back here," Jamie growled in a low whisper, but Tony blocked it out and stepped into the dark.

The night was warm, the darkness all-encompassing. It felt as if it were wrapping around him and separating him from the rest of the world. It was a sensation he was used to, often finding it hard to relate to people, especially in a group setting where there were too many dynamics for him to follow.

Stepping further away from the door, he found a comfort in the night. It quieted his racing thoughts, which, as they so often did, caught up with him as the day drew to a close. Adapting to what was happening was a skill he had developed over the years, but it was nothing more than a delay. The sensory overload would always come back to him.

He could hear them calling his name from inside the cabin, but the group could have been on the other side of the trees they sounded so distant.

Tony stopped, sniffing the air, as the foulness of the odor that hung there broke through the noise, silencing it in a way he had never before experienced.

The odor was horrid, the musky scent of stale body odor, with a heavier component that Tony could not place, but felt would be something how a body would smell if left untouched and discovered only after several weeks had gone by. It was a cloying aroma that made his eyes water and his throat burn. He could taste it even when consciously breathing through his nose, an act that was made harder by his body's sudden need for copious amounts of oxygen. His heart started racing again, and the hairs on his body stood erect. The tingling sensation was back, only now it was running down his spine, cascading like an icy waterfall, leaving behind it a path of frozen flesh.

Pulling out his phone, Tony fumbled with the lock, as the darkness suddenly took on the menacing appearance it held for the others still inside. Using the light generated by his screen, Tony looked around, trying to cut a line of sight in the blackness of the night. The phone had little effect but provided some comfort. The hefted fire iron also went some way toward the same end, an emotional support weapon, ready to use at a moment's notice. Not that Tony had ever been in a fight, or anything close to one, unless arguing with his sister counted.

The aroma didn't change. With each step, it remained constant, as if it had descended around the cabin, consuming it like a cloud.

Something crunched, and Tony jumped, spinning around. The sounds came again, louder. He raised his arm straight above his head, ready to strike, but nothing came. He waited, lost in the stench.

A few moments passed, and he was still alone. Turning back the way he had been heading, it came again. Looking down, he saw it, glinting under the light of his phone: shards of glass, shattered from the broken perimeter lights that had been hung on the wall. Four in total were smashed, the entire stretch of decking littered with shards that twinkled like fallen stars, yanked from the heavens by whatever had attacked the cabin.

Fear began to consume him, but Tony pushed on. He had made up his mind to check out the cabin for damage, and that is what he would do. A few paces further and he saw the railings that lined the outside of the deck were smashed and broke, the wood ripped from its fixtures and flung in all directions. Snapped and splintered, whatever had come through had cut a path of destruction.

Tony's blood chilled and he shivered, despite the relative warmth of the night. He approached the corner of the cabin and stopped. He could hear something, a groan, or so it sounded.

Raspy inhalations that did not just bring him to a stop but froze him completely to the spot. Unable to move forward or backward, his mind conjured up images of all manner of creatures. He saw a large black bear pawing at the rear door, its blood-stained maw pulled back into a snarl, its hunger far from sated.

Tony shook his head, forcing the image to dissolve. He was allowing his imagination to control him. He took a steeling breath and peered around the corner. The darkness seemed complete behind the cabin, and the stench seemed to carry on a sudden breeze. Tony willed his eyes to adjust, sure he could make something out of the shroud, but then the hand fell on his shoulder.

The scream leaped from his lungs and he spun around, slipping to the floor as he swatted out hopelessly at whatever it was he thought stood behind him.

He hit the deck hard, his arm snagging on a jagged piece of wood. He heard his shirt rip, followed by the piercing pain like an injection from an oversized needle.

"Oh my God, oh my God, Tony, I'm sorry," Stella cried. "It's me, it's just me."

"My arm," Tony said as he pulled himself free of the skewer that had embedded itself in his body.

"I came to see if you were alright. Oh, I'm so sorry, here, let me help you up." Stella reached out and tried to haul Tony to his feet.

Her good intentions only caused further agony as the wood snapped, freeing Tony from the decking, but not from the foreign object in his forearm.

He winced as he got to his feet. "We need to get inside," he grunted against the pain.

"Why, what did you see?" Stella asked her arm around his waist, moving as if she expected to take his weight and aide his retreat.

"I don't know, but we are safer inside," Tony answered. "Besides, I need someone to take a look at my arm."

Tony lifted his injured limb, and Stella turned her cellphone onto it. The sight of the wound and the freely flowing blood made Stella shudder, and for a moment, their roles were reversed, and it was Tony that needed to take her weight, to keep her from falling.

"Come on," Tony said. "We'll help each other."

Tony took one last look over his shoulder, but the darkness had changed again. The grumbling sounds of labored breath where gone, and the stench that hung, while still present, was far less obvious than it had been just moments before.

The others were waiting for them, standing around the door with nervous expressions etched onto their faces. Even Ricky had moved closer to the group and allowed himself to wear a look of mild concern.

They all startled when the pair appeared and jumped backward as the two charged over the threshold, collapsing to the floor.

"Oh my God, what happened?" Jamie cried out when she saw the blood leaking from her brother's arm.

"I fell. The decking around the cabin is trashed," Tony spoke through gritted teeth. Now that he was in an illuminated room, he could see the damage the fall had done to his arm. With that came the knowledge of how bad it was, and riding on the coattails of that understanding was pain.

The splinter, not that it could be called a splinter, as Tony had seen smaller pieces of wood used to make a fire, had penetrated his arm just above the wrist. The weight of his fall had driven it a good six inches into his arm, tearing the flesh part way along the intrusion point. Blood flowed from the wound like a crimson flood, the rich-colored fluid streaking along his uninjured flesh before dripping to the floor. The rest of the wooden shard protruded from Tony's forearm like a jagged piece of bone.

"Hold still, we need to take it out," Colin said.

"No, you can't," Jamie shrieked. "What if it gets infected or leaves a splinter?"

"We can't leave it in there like that, and we need to stop the bleeding," Colin replied, crouching down to take a closer look at the injury.

Tony sat on the floor, sweat dripping from him as if he had just finished a Zumba class. His skin was pale, and his head spun from the sight of all the blood gushing from his body. He knew he wasn't going to die from the wound, but he could not stop his mind from running away from him.

He placed his head back against the wall and closed his eyes, willing the shard out of his body.

"It's going to be fine, Tony." Stella crouched down beside him, laying a hand on his shoulder. "You feel like you're burning up."

"He doesn't like the sight of blood. He never has," Jamie said, her words hurried from the concern that was consuming her. "I'll get a cloth."

She turned and hurried away, while Colin gently touched the protruding shard. The moment he made contact, waves of electric pain were sent shooting through Tony's body, as if Colin was somehow a conductor of some sort and his contact with the wood completed the circuit, sending power shooting through everything along the connection line.

"Sorry." Colin removed his hand and held them up in surrender.

"Oh Jesus, it's just a splinter," Ricky said as he opened another beer.

"Then why not put down the beer and help us for once?" Colin snarled, turning to glare up at Ricky.

"I'm good, thanks," he replied, taking a long, slow drink.

"Jackass," Colin muttered as he turned back to Tony.

It was obvious that Ricky heard the comment because he crumpled the can in his grip and turned back to the kitchen, not bothering to move to one side as Jamie came back with a damp towel.

She glared at him but kept her mouth shut.

"Here, hold this against his head." She handed the wet cloth to Stella, who obliged without hesitation. "It's going to be okay, Tony."

Tony had started to shake, his breaths coming quicker and quicker as shock started to hit him.

"I've got to do it," Colin said. "It's in deep."

"Can't we just drive him to a hospital or something?" Jamie asked, her eyes brimming with tears.

"We still don't know what was out there, or if it has damaged the car," Colin answered. "I can go give it a look."

"No," Tony groaned through gritted teeth. "Do it." He opened his eyes and looked at Colin, holding his gaze with a fierce glare.

"On three," Colin said, positioning himself. "Have that towel ready. Hold him down."

Colin addressed Stella and Jamie in turn, and both reacted without hesitation. Tony closed his eyes and leaned back into the wall, trying to relax as much as he could. He was cold, his arm alternating between feeling totally numb and as if it had been set on fire.

"One, two …" Colin counted down and pulled the wooden shard before he reached the three.

Tony gritted his teeth but could not contain all the sounds his brain demanded he make to express his agony.

He felt the wood shift inside him, withdrawing with a slow, wet feeling, leaving behind it the sensation of loss. Tony could feel the blood flowing faster than ever, while his arm felt strangely hollow from where the foreign object had been embedded.

"Almost got it," Colin said, his words strained from the focus he needed to give the extraction.

Tony opened his eyes and peeked at the procedure. The bloody shard was dripping with gore, and what looked to be chunks of meat hanging from the splintered edges. Colin's hands were likewise covered with blood.

A rush of warm air hit Tony, and he felt the world begin to fade to black, the charging swarm of unconsciousness. A final blast of pain chased it away as Colin pulled the shard free, and the towel was clamped down and around his arm by Stella.

"We got it, Tony, we got it," Jaime cried, relief washing over her.

"That's a nasty wound. We need to clean it before we bandage it up," Colin said, looking over to Ricky for assistance. "Can you look for something to clean the wound with?"

Ricky looked at Colin for a moment and then nodded, with an air of reluctance about him. He came back a short time later with an unlabeled bottle of liquor.

"It's all I can find," he said, handing the three-quarter-full bottle to Colin.

"It'll do," Colin said, unwrapping the towel to take a look at the wound.

The long puncture had already slowed its bleed, and although a tear in the flesh would most likely need stitches, Colin didn't think it was a life-threatening injury.

"This will sting," he said as he poured a generous amount of booze over the wound.

Tony closed his eyes and hissed at the sharp sting. The pain was less in comparison to what he had just experienced and so he swallowed it down, clenching his jaw until the worst of it passed.

With the wound wrapped up in a fresh towel and taped together with a roll of duct tape found in the kitchen drawer, Tony began to calm and regain his composure.

He got up from the floor and avoided looking at the blood smears over the floor. His clothes were also covered, while he was also acutely aware of how hard he was sweating. Dropping into the sofa, he let out a long sigh.

"This is a fun trip." His tone was flat and other than Jamie, nobody knew how to take the comment.

Jamie laughed and Tony smiled, which gave the signal to the others his suggestion had been light-hearted, and with that, they all collapsed back onto the sofas, Ricky the only one of them still with a drink in his hand.

'There's still something out there," Jamie said after a while.

"Whatever it was, it was gone when I was looking for it," Tony said, remembering the presence he had felt in the darkness, and how it had disappeared once Stella reached him.

"It was probably just a bear. It was already getting dark when we arrived. We probably startled it or something," Colin offered. "A bear would explain the damage and the pounding on the door."

"A bear wouldn't do that," Stella said from the sofa.

"Have you ever seen an angry bear in the wild?" Colin asked, his tone neutral and composed.

"Well, no, but I mean, that decking is destroyed," Stella said, stumbling over her words.

"Well, they are killing machines. They can weight over 1,300 pounds and can kill a moose with a single hit. They could easily tear this place down if something drove them to it." Colin reeled off the facts, not to sound smart, but to emphasize his point.

"I guess, but I don't know, it just doesn't feel like a bear." Stella shook her head as she spoke, going along with the explanation, but clearly not sold on it.

"Maybe it was Bigfoot," Ricky slurred, coughing out a heavy drunken laugh.

Tony raised his head and stared at Ricky, who stopped laughing and stared back.

"Holy shit, you believe me. Jesus Christ, I knew you were stupid, but fuck me if you believe in that fucking ape story." Ricky laughed again, only now all traces of his awkward humor were gone. He mocked Tony with his laugh.

"Leave him alone," Jamie snarled.

Colin shot to his feet. He spun around in a blur of motion and grabbed the shocked Ricky by the shirt, bunching the material into his two closed fists.

"Hey, hey, easy man, I'm just fucking around," Ricky said, smiling nervously.

Colin didn't loosen his grip and kept his face pressed close to Ricky's. It was only when Jamie walked over and placed her arms on his that he let go. Turning to face his girlfriend, he forgot Ricky, who took several quick paces backward.

"I've had enough of you nervous fuckers," he said as he straightened his shirt. The bravado was stripped from his voice, and all that was left was the pain of being shown up. "I'm going to bed, Stella, come on."

Ricky turned and stormed toward the main bedroom, making it close to the door before he stopped and turned around. "Stella, I said come on."

Stella remained sitting on the sofa. With her friends around her, she stared down the room toward Ricky. She sat up straight and shook her head. A slight motion at first, but clear enough so that when the words came, they were merely a confirmation.

"No, I'm going to sit here for a while," she said.

Tony could feel Stella tremble as she stood up to her bully of a boyfriend and wanted to put his arm around her for support, but he couldn't. His head was still fogged by pain and moving too much hurt.

But he watched as Ricky's face as the concept of rejection dawned on him. His face brimmed with rage but was quickly tempered by Colin, who still stood, and merely had to turn in Ricky's direction for the message to become clear enough.

Ricky stood his ground for a moment but lowered his gaze. He waited for a few moments, plunging the cabin into an awkward silence before he stormed into the bedroom and slammed the door.

"You sure know how to pick them," Jamie said to Stella after a few moments later.

Stella said nothing but sat back on the sofa beside Tony who himself remained equally silent. He stared at the fireplace, watching it as if it was lit, and the dancing flames were holding him under their hypnotic sway.

For a moment, Tony looked across at Stella and willed her to look up, to meet his gaze. He wanted to know if she had felt what he had felt, to ask if she had also sensed the presence of something massive outside the cabin. He didn't dare. His mind was drunk with pain, and Ricky's scornful words echoed in his ears, suppressing his inclination to speak of anything that may make him sound crazy.

He knew what people thought of him and what they called him behind his back. He trusted those close to him, but Ricky had him on edge, and that sat uncomfortably around him. Like an ill-fitting sweatshirt, it felt wrong, but at the same time, Tony knew he had no right, no power, to remove the man. To take a sweatshirt off and walk around bare-chested was a thought even more uncomforting to Tony's racing mind.

"Tony, are you sure you don't want to go to the hospital?" Jamie asked, her words overflowing with concern for her big brother.

"No, I'm fine. It's a long drive, we've all been drinking, and besides, it doesn't hurt too bad anymore. I think it's stopped bleeding already," Tony lied, hoping the others couldn't see his arm throbbing with pain, the same way he imagined it.

"Okay, but if it gets bad, we're taking you, and I don't want to hear any arguments from you," Jamie said sternly. Having grown up with a brother like Tony, she had learned at an early age that she would need to watch out for him. He was too kind and soft to survive in the world without someone watching over him.

"Well, it's getting kinda late. I think we should hit the hay and see what the morning brings. If everything is well and good, your friends should arrive, and we can get on with the fun," Colin said, looking at Jamie.

"I guess, it's just … are you sure you're okay?" Jamie stared at Tony, as if somehow she could see through the physical part of him and into his emotions.

"I'm fine," Tony said, wincing a little as he repositioned himself on the sofa.

"It's cool, you guys go to bed. I'll stay with Tony. I don't think I could sleep anyway, not after everything that happened tonight," Stella said, looking around the room as if terrified of the dark secrets the shadows may hold.

"If it's that bad, why are you with him?" Jamie asked.

"I don't mean Ricky. Well …" Stella paused and lowered her gaze. "I mean with everything outside. You know, the bear, or whatever it was."

"That thing is long gone now. Besides, it couldn't break in just now, so I think it must have lost interest in us. There are easier pickings in the woods," Colin offered, stretching as he got to his feet.

"I guess you're right, but I still won't be able to sleep. You guys go, get some rest. We'll be fine here, won't we, Tony?" Stella forced a smile on her face.

"Yeah, I guess," Tony answered, more confused than ever.

Jamie and Colin stood and collected the empty cans and bottles, dumping them in the kitchen sink before saying their final goodnights and disappearing into the back bedroom. The silence created by their departure was loud but comforting.

"It wasn't a bear, was it?" Stella said after a while.

"No, I don't think it was," Tony replied, unable to take his eyes away from the window and the darkness that lay beyond.

CHAPTER FIVE

A drop of cold water hit her burning skin and Tammy screamed. Her legs were still on fire from where she had been dragged along the road.

Her head ached also, and the reverberations of her scream only served to make it worse, for the echo told her more about the size of the space she was trapped in.

Her jaw ached, and her mouth tasted of blood. She could feel a large chunk of her tongue was loose in her mouth. She bit it as she tried to scream just as the bat connected with her face. She wasn't sure it was a bat; it could have been a pipe or anything else. She never saw it coming.

"Hello?" she called again into the darkness. Her words were muffled and slurred. She tried to move, but her bonds were too tight.

Someone had tied her hands behind her back, and then connected the rope down to her ankles. The rope had not been long enough, so Tammy was bent backward at a painful angle, her back screaming with cramp as her body sought some meager scrap of comfort.

Tammy knew she was going to die. She wept because she didn't want to die alone. She had no idea where her friend was. Susan had waited in the car while she went into the store to ask for directions. It had been Susan's scream that made her turn away from the creepy man behind the register. She had seen two men reaching into her car, grabbing at her friend.

Her first thought was a kidnapping; a terribly executed, clumsy kidnapping attempt. She turned back to the register, her mouth open to scream at the man, ordering him to do something or call somebody.

Then the blow came.

The first was to her gut, which saw her double over in pain, vomiting up the potato chips she and Susan had declared to be a viable lunch. She raised her head, pain exploding, and darkness was all that followed.

She had not seen any daylight since. She woke up shivering, conscious of her own body, stripped down to her underwear. Her first moment of panic came upon waking. Convinced she had been buried alive, she screamed and thrashed until the pain of her injuries plunged her back into the icy numbness of unconsciousness.

When she woke, she forced her mind to stay calm. She strained and listened. She could hear people, voices. She had screamed, and that was when the real nightmare began.

The people she could hear answered her cries. A moment of hope turned into a blood-chilling reality when the words they whispered to her finally filtered through to her brain.

She was a prisoner, and wherever she was now, it was just a holding cell. They had other plans for her.

At one point, Tammy was sure she had heard Susan scream, but whatever it was fell swiftly silent and did not rise up again.

Time had lost all meaning. Tammy knew it was early afternoon when they pulled into the store parking lot, but since then, any amount of time could have passed by. She was oblivious to it. The only thing she knew for certain was that time was running out.

The light was sudden and blinding. The hands that grabbed her were rough and unyielding. The strong grip belonged to an equally strong frame, for Tammy's captor hauled her effortlessly into the air and flung her over his shoulder.

The man stunk of grease and a particularly musky body odor that made Tammy gag and struggle, if not to escape the awful stench.

"Quiet. They'd prefer you whole, but don't test me, cunt," the voice growled.

It was night, or so Tammy reasoned, for after the blinding light was removed from her eyes, she found herself once again surrounded by darkness. Only now, it was different.

"This one's a live wire," the voice said again, speaking to some unknown accomplice.

"This one's kind of broken. She's just all limp. I prefer it when they fight." The voice was not as gruff and made Tammy think of someone younger.

"Sure she's not dead?" a gruff voice growled.

"Nope, just broken. Wanna swap?" the young voice asked.

"Just put her in the back. You know they don't like it when we rough 'em up," Gruff instructed, clearly the one in charge of things.

Tammy was conscious of being carried, and moving from inside to out, for the cold chill of the night made her skin scream.

"Let me go," she whimpered, the power she had hoped to find in her voice nowhere to be heard.

She didn't know if her captor had heard her, but he gave no answer, and merely carried on walking.

"Tammy?" a weak voice called out through the darkness.

The sound of her words, so hollow and afraid, was enough to break Tammy. She had almost come to accept her own fate, and if anything, felt relieved at the knowledge she would not die buried alive in a box somewhere. But as she heard her friend, so close and yet so far away, also committed to a fate she felt responsible for, she broke.

It had been Tammy's insistence that Susan join them for the weekend. Susan had said no repeatedly, but Tammy always had to get her own way, and she did with Susan too. She broke her down and now she had signed her death warrant.

"Susan, Susan, I'm sorry," Tammy began, her words ending abruptly as she was thrown backward.

Blind, and unable to tell when the impact was likely to occur, Tammy screamed, the wind rushing out of her lungs when she hit the hard surface not long after her launch.

There was another thud beside her and she knew that it was Susan. Two more thuds soon followed, and when the engine started, Tammy figured out where they were. The eerie red glow offered by the truck's tail lights merely confirmed it.

Rolling over, trying to loosen her bonds a little, Tammy rolled to find her friend.

"Susan?" Tammy spoke, assuming they were alone in the back of the truck. "Susan?"

"Tammy? I'm afraid." Susan sounded like a child, calling out from their bed because the dark was too terrifying to face alone.

"Me too, but listen, we can escape. Are you tied up?" Tammy asked. The bonds around her arms had loosened somewhat, but nowhere near enough to let her escape.

"Yes, but I can probably get out of it."

The truck roared to life and took off, bumping and bouncing down the road, throwing the two young women around. The noisy engine and the unpaved road made it impossible to continue any conversation.

When the truck finally came to a stop, Tammy ached all over from the battering her body had been dealt by the truck bed. The engine shut off and all she could hear was Susan's weeping, which was swiftly drowned out by her own.

The front doors slammed and heavy footsteps slapped against the ground. The truck shuddered and then groaned as the tailboard was unlocked and lowered.

Susan screamed first, and Tammy heard her friend's body drag across the truck bed. A strong hand grabbed her by the ankles and pulled hard. Tammy was yanked from the truck, her bruised body crying out in pain as the sharp edge of the tailgate sliced through her thigh.

Tammy steeled herself, and when the man grabbed her upper arm, meaning to pull her to her feet, she struck out. Raising her knee, she connected with the man's flabby gut. He grunted, and she struck again, screaming as she drove her knee into his ribs.

The man dropped to the ground, and for a moment, Tammy was free. Lost in the dark, the ground soft and wet beneath her feet, she turned a sharp circle, looking for anything. Her mind was racing. Escape was her only thought.

She blocked out all other things.

The truck!

The thought hit her in a sudden moment of inspiration. She didn't think about how she would drive with her arms tied. She needn't have considered that far ahead, for she made it all of three steps before the man's meaty hand clamped on her shoulder. She was spun around and just as she completed her rotation, a giant fist connected with her jaw. Tammy's head snapped back the way it had come from, hurling her into unconsciousness once more.

Tammy came too on her cold ground. It smelled of mud and pine needles. She was aware that she had been placed on all fours, and of the presence behind her.

All manner of thoughts went flooding through her mind. Beside her, Susan cried out.

"Please, don't do this." Her voice was broken, the words hard to decipher.

The men said nothing for a second, then there was a resounding clap, a hand making hard, open-palmed contact with the skin. It was unmistakable.

"That's right, little thing. Piss yourself good," the young voice growled.

Tammy heard her friend's whimpers and her bladder lose control. She bit down on her lip as she fought back the near overwhelming urge to relieve herself also. She wouldn't give them the satisfaction.

"They like that. It helps them smell your fear." The man finished talking with a bark. A genuine bark, like a dog, mad with rabies.

"What are you going to do with us?" Tammy asked. Her head felt thick from the punch, her lips thick and swollen.

"Oh, it's not what we are going to do to you, honey. Trust me, you'd enjoy that, but this … this you won't enjoy at all." The man Tammy attacked was still winded, but she didn't have the energy to fight him again.

Tammy felt something cold prod into her lower back. She felt the cool steel and knew that the man was holding a gun to her.

"Get up and start walking," he growled, jabbing the barrel of whatever weapon he was holding sharply into her flesh.

Tammy couldn't speak. Her resolve had crumbled, and all she could do was drag herself to her feet and start walking.

She hugged herself, wrapping her arms tight around her body, the cold air chilling her near-nude body to the bone. As her eyes adjusted to the darkness, she could make out Susan beside her, stripped in the same way as she was, only, rather than being lead at gunpoint, Susan's captor had a rope around her throat and lead her like an animal on a leash.

Tammy realized they were in the woods but could not understand why. They were being led deeper, rising up an incline that caused her calves to burn. She didn't stop. She couldn't. While she couldn't fight back any longer, she was still not yet ready to die.

The cold ground sent a spreading wave of numbness through Tammy's lower legs. Her calves felt as if they were burning from cramp the cold was so intense. She stumbled twice, and the second time, the man left her on the ground.

"Tie them up," he addressed his companion. "Be quick about it."

"Do you smell that?" the younger voice asked.

Tammy did, but she would not give the man an answer. The stench was strong and had been growing stronger for the last few minutes. It smelled like rot and body odor. It was thick and horrid, the sort of stench that made you want to breathe through your mouth so as not to smell it, only to then make you realize that you were eating whatever the foul stench was.

"That's why I said tie them up quickly. They're already on their way." Tammy thought she heard a touch of urgency in the fat man's voice.

Things were not going according to plan.

"Then let's just leave 'em here. We'll never make it back to the truck if we stop to tie 'em up." The young voice was not so much tinged with urgency but rather laced with fear.

"No, we need to get them ready. Can't take the chance they'll escape. We need to keep them things happy." The large man had moved, his voice no longer coming from in front of where Tammy rested, once again reduced to her hands and knees.

"What are you doing? Let me go!" Susan's voice was sudden and shrill.

"Shut up. It won't be long now," the fat man growled.

His hands grabbed Tammy roughly from the front, hauling her to his feet. She knew she did not mistake his hands running over her chest as he got her steady, pulling her bra low enough for her nipples to spring free. The cold air had made them painful, and Tammy winced as they scraped against the top of her bra.

The man said nothing, but the pattern of his breathing told Tammy all she needed to know about how he felt.

Before she knew what was happening, her arms were freed from their bonds but pulled behind her back. The brute spun her around and dragged her backward, stretching her aching shoulders to the point of dislocation.

Scrambling backward, trying to keep her balance, Tammy slammed into something and let out a groan. The rough bark of the tree rubbed at her flesh like sandpaper.

"Let me go." The fire returned to her as she realized what was happening. Her hands were bound again, tied behind the tree, immobilizing her. She struggled and felt something tear in her left shoulder. The pain was intense and flared through her like an explosion.

She dropped to her knees, but the bonds were too tight, and her right shoulder gave an audible pop as it came free from its socket.

Unable to hold herself anymore, Tammy wet herself, listening with growing shame as the sound of her urination splashed onto the mud around her feet.

"Atta girl." The fat man ran his hands down her body on last time before turning to his young assistant. "Time to get going. Grab that gear and hurry."

Then they were alone. Tammy heard the two men stumble through the trees, the light from torches showing the hurried and frantic path they chose to follow.

"Why did they do this?" Susan cried, her voice little more than a whisper, her throat damaged as a result of the crude leash that had been fastened around her throat.

"I don't know," Tammy replied. "Wait, did you hear that?"

"Hear what?" Susan asked, her form nothing but a shadow in the night.

"I thought I heard something," Tammy said.

"Perhaps they are coming back, coming to let us go," Susan replied hopefully.

Tammy opened her mouth to say something, but the forest moved around her, silencing her words.

At first, she thought she was seeing things, her battered brain playing tricks on her by moving the shadows around them. Then came the stench, and the low guttural growl that seemed to echo through the trees. Yellow eyes flashed and the ground trembled. The eyes blinked and when they opened again, they rose up into the night, as if flying away, while the growl ended in a snarl with large fangs gleaming in the night.

The creature, whatever it was, stood behind Susan, hidden from her view. She never saw her end coming.

"Oh my God, that sm—" she never finished her sentence for her head was removed from her body in the blink of an eye.

Tammy watch the head all but disappear as a black limb swung around and decapitated her friend. Susan's body remained on its feet, supported by its restraints. Blood jettisoned into the air like a fountain set to a piece of music. Shooting high, shining in the moonlight, each burst grew steadily weaker until there was no power left and the blood merely spilled from the remaining stump of neck.

The creature emerged from the darkness, closing in on Susan's blood-drenched body. It stood taller than a man, Tammy guessed at least seven feet, maybe closer to eight. Its body was covered in long, black fur. It looked like a gorilla caught in the midst of an evolutionary jump. The creature stopped, bent down, and sniffed the corpse. Satisfied, it grabbed the body and tore it in half as if the flesh and bone were made of nothing but damp tissue paper.

Tammy shat herself as she heard the wet squelch of her friend's insides spilling to the ground. This was followed by the crunch of bone and smack of hungry jaws swallowing down the warm treat.

The creature discarded the leftover scraps of Susan-meat the way one might throw away a chip packet once the contents were gone. It sniffed the air, as the scent of defecation tantalized its taste buds. Its movements were slow, almost thoughtful. It turned to face Tammy, its eyes burning with furious hunger.

It growled once more, the lips peeled back as if retracting up into its skin, revealing blood-stained teeth. The most prominent of which were the four, three-inch-long incisors. The creature closed in and Tammy saw blood dripping from the fangs like venom. She opened her mouth to scream but the monster tore her head from her body and threw it through the trees with a casual disinterest.

Tammy's body fell into its restraints, her severed neck lurching forward, spewing warm gouts of blood over the creature's fur. Curious, the thing took hold of the body with both hands and pulled it away from the tree. Both shoulders dislocated with a crack before the rope finally snapped free. The beast stopped and sniffed the air before it returned deeper into the trees, dragging the still-bleeding corpse behind it.

CHAPTER SIX

Tony woke as if he was rising through treacle. The dream world held to him, twice dragging him back down the very moment he broke the surface of waking. When he finally came around, all he knew was pain. He half-sat, half-lay on the sofa, and his neck refused to move, having seemingly locked into place at an awkward, pain-inducing angle.

Moving slowly, aware of something else pressing down on him, Tony managed to raise his head and assume a normal posture. Looking down, he saw Stella curled up with her head resting against him. His arm was draped over her shoulder, and the sudden realization that his hand lay on her breast caused him to jerk it away. Embarrassed, he wondered if she had noticed.

His movement caused Stella to stir, opening her eyes with a flutter. She looked up and smiled at Tony as if their positions were the most natural thing in the world. "Good morning," she said smiling, and Tony felt the butterflies start to dance in his stomach.

"Morning," he answered.

Stella sat up and stretched, while Tony felt sad for losing the comfort of her body resting against his own.

The memories of the previous night began to replay in his head, as they had, to a lesser degree, in his dreams. Before he could say anything, however, the door to one of the bedrooms opened and Ricky came walking out, his hair wet from the shower, a towel hanging over his shoulders. He was only dressed from the waist down. Tony looked at him and understood why. He was threatened and wanted to show his physique. Last night had seen Colin emerge as the alpha male in the group. It was a role that Tony held no interest in, but it was a dance he had seen play out in several different social circles in his first year at college.

Beside him, Tony felt Stella stiffen. She jumped to her feet as if embarrassed, or had been caught doing something illegal.

"Hey, honey," she said, her words erratic with adrenaline.

Ricky glanced at Tony, but his eyes soon turned to Stella. His gaze became a scowl and soon thereafter a look of pure, unadulterated rage consumed him.

"You never came to bed last night. I wondered if I just slept through it, but I see you got very comfy sleeping somewhere else last night."

Ricky's hands opened and clenched, never relaxing.

"What, no, no, it wasn't like that. We were both exhausted by what happened last night. I must have just passed out." Stella gave a nervous laugh. "I don't even remember falling asleep."

She glanced down at Tony, who understood what she was looking for. "It's true, man, we just woke up a second ago. Must have passed out." Tony fumbled his words while inwardly debating whether he should rise to his feet or if that would be viewed as a challenge somehow.

"Yeah, I'm sure," Ricky said, scowling at them both. His jaw clenched, and his eyes narrowed, but he turned and moved back toward the kitchen area.

Tony breathed a sigh of relief, but Ricky stopped mid-stride and turned back to face them.

"You fucking this retard?" he growled, staring straight at Stella.

Stella said nothing but walked towards Ricky, who face held a reptilian smirk at seeing her come toward him. It flew away when Stella raised her hand and slapped him hard across the face.

"You're a bastard," she screamed at him. "I'm sorry," she said to Tony, looking over her shoulder at him and then ran toward the door.

She fumbled with the lock as she fought back tears, but broke free from the house and ran out into the early morning.

Tony jumped up from the sofa, just as his sister and Colin emerged from the bedroom, their eyes still crusted with sleep.

Tony moved to the door, but someone grabbed him by the arm and spun him around. He came to a stop with his nose pressed against Ricky's.

"She's mine, you understand me? Touch her, and I fuck you up," Ricky spoke with clenched teeth, sweat sheening on his forehead while his face paled in color as the blood drained away. He was lost to his rage, but Tony was not going to leave Stella alone outside.

Tony had never been in a fight, not even close to one, but he balled his fists, set his stance, and as Ricky twisted his grip on Tony's arm, he shoved the man backward, using his closed fists to drive his power into Ricky's shoulders.

Stunned, Ricky stumbled back, tripped, and fell onto his ass, landing in a messy heap on the floor.

"What's going on?" Jamie asked, suddenly awake and alert.

Tony didn't answer her but turned toward the door. He heard footsteps behind him and was ready to swing the first angry punch of his life. Hands grabbed him again, but he knew the touch was not Ricky's. His anger slid away, and he turned to stare at his sister.

"Tony, where's Stella? What happened here?" Jamie asked.

"She ran away. This asshole accused us of ..." Tony froze, catching himself as he became unable to explain any further. His mind was a jumbled mess of too many different scenarios playing out all at once.

To Tony, everything was a puzzle, and he needed time to piece things together before he could fully understand them. Now, with so many puzzles all jumbled together, his brain felt as if it had been scrambled.

Jamie nodded. She knew enough.

"You, stay here," she instructed Tony. "Colin, watch him, and you, you son of a bitch, stay away from my friend, and my brother."

Nobody argued with Jamie. As petite and sweet as she was, two of the three men left in the cabin had experience with getting on her bad side and knew better than to voluntarily take a trip there.

Leaving the men to drown in their own devices, Jamie hurried outside to find her friend.

***

It was darker out than it looked from inside, and the cold air of early morning bit at Jamie's skin through the thin pajamas she wore.

Standing on the deck, she looked left and right for a sign of her friend. All she saw was the damage from the night before. Seeing it with her own eyes, she understood why Tony and Stella had been so spooked.

"Stella?" Jamie called, looking over toward the car, wondering if her friend was hiding there.

No answer came so she walked down the front steps, flinching as her bare feet hit the cold forest ground.

There was no obvious sign as to which direction Stella had fled, and after finding the car empty and no immediate trace of her friend to be seen, Jamie turned and went back inside. She half-expected the guys to be fighting and find furniture overturned and blood splattered over the walls. Her shock at finding them sitting and standing in silence must have shown on her face.

"It's all civil in here," Colin said.

"Did you find Stella?" Tony asked, his voice laced with concern.

"No, she's not in the car or outside the cabin. I guess she ran into the woods or something," Jamie answered.

"I'm going to go look for her." Tony stood up and grabbed his jacket.

"We'll all go," Colin agreed, glancing at Ricky, who still sat in silence.

"If we each take a side and walk through the woods, we'll find her." Jamie looked at her brother as she spoke, finding herself reassuring him. Tony certainly looked to be the most worried of the group.

Ricky said nothing, but followed alone, moving straight ahead and into the trees without waiting for them to come to an agreement regarding how far or long they would go between checking in with one another.

"I'll go this way," Tony said, heading over toward the car and around to the right of the cabin. "I'll meet you back here in ten minutes. If you find her, send a text." He held up his phone, waving it in the air as if the visual display was needed for the others to understand what he meant.

"What if you lose the signal?" Jamie asked.

"I won't," Tony replied confidently, before turning away from the group.

"Colin, you go left, and I'll go round back and look there." While she would never admit to enjoying the role of leader, it was a position that came naturally to Jamie. From looking after her brother, watching over him for so long, she had developed traits and skills that became so ingrained she could no longer see them for what they were.

"What about ... whatever it was that did that?" Colin pointed at the trashed deck.

"That bear is long gone by now. Besides, Stella is out there alone." Jamie would not be discouraged. Her friend needed her help.

She left Colin and hurried around the cabin, her mind now only half-concerned about what could be lurking in the pre-dawn shadows.

Tony hurried through the trees, moving beyond the car and into the woods without hesitation. His mind was set on finding Stella, and that was what he would do. The puzzles didn't matter if Stella wasn't there with him.

He didn't know exactly what he felt for her, but it was something that had been building for many years. Yet it took seeing her with Ricky for him to realize just how badly he wanted her in his life.

Having grown up with a protective family, Tony never understood how different he was. It was only when he left for school that he became more aware of how he looked at the world and daily life differently than other people. He ran on patterns. Everything he did, he saw a pattern in it. He could apply that same pattern to everything, approaching it like a puzzle, slotting the steps into place to get to the end goal. It meant he took his time. He never rushed, but when he was done, he was always done. He never had to redo assignments or projects. It was right the first time, every time.

Now, he could see the pattern with Stella; he could see how she needed to be saved. It was just a matter of finding the right steps and putting that puzzle together.

He didn't have to look for long before he heard sobbing. He could recognize Stella's voice no matter what sound it made. There was a tone to it that spoke to him. Normally, hearing it made him nervous, but there was a pain in her cry that made him feel angry and protective.

As he moved through the trees, veering to his left, he wondered if that was how Jamie felt about him.

Stella was sitting on the ground, her back pressed against a tree. With her knees drawn up to her chest, and her long hair loose-flowing from her bowed head, she looked like a creature of the forest.

Tony moved toward her, and Stella bolted upright. Anger and hatred flashed in her eyes, and she held a broken tree branch across her lap like a club.

Her eyes met Tony's and her face softened. The rage fell away and the pain returned.

Tony walked closer to her, moving slowly and carefully, trying to process how best to handle the emotion that was overflowing from her. Stella solved the puzzle for him. She rose to her feet and fell into his arms. Her hands locked around his neck and their bodies pressed close together.

Even though her body felt cold, almost frozen, there was a warmth that rushed over Tony as they stood there. He didn't want to let her go. There was a chance he wouldn't have, had his eyes not found something a short distance deeper into the trees.

"What is that?" Tony asked as Stella turned to look also.

"I don't know," Stella replied with a hitch.

"It looks like a car."

Together, they walked deeper into the woods, their hands still connected, heat still flowing from one to the other.

The car was nestled neatly between the trees. Its windows were shattered, the driver-side doors, both front and back, had been torn away. The roof was caved in, as if something heavy had been dropped onto it, and the driver's seat looked as if something had tried to rip it free but given up on it, the job half done.

"The plates are from out of state," Tony said as he used the flashlight app on his phone to examine the car. "Pretty new too; it's last year's model."

"How did it get out here and so beat up?" Stella asked, backing away from the wreck as if it were some bad luck charm or poisonous snake that could pounce on them at any time.

"I have no idea. There's no damage that looks like it came from a crash," Tony mused, scratching his chin.

"Why would someone drive a car so deep into the woods and just abandon it here?" Stella asked. She eyed the car suspiciously.

Tony looked around them, his mind working as he tried to put another puzzle together in his mind. He discarded the pieces that remained of him and Stella. That could wait.

Working on the car, he looked the body over, and then back through the trees.

"It had to come from back that way. The way we came," he reasoned.

"What makes you so sure?" Stella asked, taking another step back. Her foot caught on something and she stumbled. Had Tony not still held her hand within his own, she would have fallen.

"Well, there's no space to turn around, so it had to drive in. It's on a straight line from the cabin, so it had to come from there. Maybe it belongs to Tammy's brother or something. I know she has three. They could have come out here, got drunk, and driven it up here. They're pretty rich, so it wouldn't make much difference to them if it got trashed." Tony didn't really feel the truth in what he was saying, and making a hypothesis was strange for him, but he could also feel that Stella needed to hear something that would calm her. The puzzles were overlapping, but he found the need to give her comfort more important than getting the right answer to the car riddle.

"Maybe. Wait, what's this?" Stella said, her attention drawn to what had caused her to stumble.

The suitcase was lying on the floor, open and partly hidden by the low-hanging leaves of a fern.

Kicking the plant away, Stella prodded the case with her foot until it was out in the open. She crouched down.

"I don't think these clothes belonged to Tammy's brother," Stella said, picking up a lacy pink thong and matching bra.

"Maybe his girlfriend," Tony said, the answer coming immediately to his mind.

"Maybe," Stella replied, her words uncertain.

Something moved in the trees. A branch cracked and fell to the floor. Both shot to attention, staring down through the trees as if the car had come to life and continued its journey straight ahead. They stared into the darkness, and while neither spoke, both saw it. The darkness hid whatever was standing there from them, but at the same time, its presence was unmistakable.

"Tony," Stella whispered, her words barely carrying to his ear.

"Yeah," Tony replied, his words just as faint.

"You … you see that, right?" she asked, as they both instinctively backed away.

Tony didn't need to answer. The thing in the shadows shifted, and they both turned to run.

Tony moved fast but ensured that he remained behind Stella. Whatever was out there had been watching them and had been doing so since they arrived.

They tore through the trees, the cabin coming into view. Stella screamed as she ran, no longer able to contain her fear. Tony chanced a look over his shoulder. The darkness had abated somewhat as dawn continued to break, but he knew that whatever it was, was still there.

Breaking from the trees and into the clearing around the cabin, they saw the others appear also, drawn by Stella's terrified screams no doubt.

Nobody spoke, there was no time for they all turned to run, following Stella's lead. Disappearing into the cabin, Tony was the last one inside, and he slammed the door, sliding down onto the floor with his back pressed against it. His mind was racing and there were too many pieces of too many puzzles for him to have to put together.

"What happened?" Jamie asked, looking from her brother to her best friend.

Having grown up with Tony, Jamie knew the signs when he needed to center himself, so she turned to Stella, the more outwardly distraught of the pair, but easily the most approachable.

"Stella, Stella, what happened?" Jamie placed her hands on her friend's shoulder.

"I'll make a cup of tea," Colin said from behind her, addressing nobody in particular.

"Out in the woods. There's a car. Clothes. Something was watching us," Stella answered, forcing the words out of either side of gasping inhalations. Her words were broken and choppy, but the sincerity behind her fear was clear.

"What is out there?" Jamie asked, a chill crawling over her body.

"A monster," Stella said the words with a suddenly serious expression. At first, Jamie thought her eyes were locked on Tony, but she soon realized they were watching the door, as if she expected it to be kicked in at any second.

"A monster? Really?" Ricky said, his voice full of scorn.

"Hun, there's no such thing as monsters," Jamie said, trying to ignore Ricky, who had just stood there the entire time.

"She's right," Tony said, speaking from his position on the floor. "I saw it too."

"Of course you did," Ricky interrupted, seemingly incapable of holding his tongue or keeping his comments to himself.

"I was out there too and didn't see no monsters. You too crazies probably saw a squirrel and got spooked." Ricky couldn't help but laugh.

He stopped quickly when Colin appeared with four mugs of tea. He conveniently skipped Ricky.

"Listen, it's been a really weird trip. We had a few drinks last night, the whole bear attacking the cabin thing; it's understandable you'd be a little spooked," Colin began, but Stella stood up, her eyes burning.

"I didn't imagine anything. There is something out there. There's a car out there too. In the trees," she said, looking from person to person.

"A suitcase full of clothes too." Tony rose from the floor near the door and walked to stand beside Stella, much to Ricky's obvious annoyance.

"Alright, hold on a second, everybody." Colin put his mug of tea on the small table that rested against the wall. "There are no monsters lurking in the woods. Maybe a few weird locals, a deer or two for sure, but no monsters. Let's just calm down, get a hold of your friends, and see where they are. Then we can take it all from there."

Jamie nodded in agreement, and Ricky said nothing, heading off to the kitchen to make his own drink. Tony and Stella looked at one another.

"We didn't imagine it," Stella whispered to him, her voice sounded sullen, like a scolded child.

"No," Tony said, his own voice low. He knew it would be hard to convince the others. Even he was starting to doubt what they had seen. It made no sense, no matter how certain he was of it. There was no logical explanation. At least, nothing beyond shadows and imagination. "But, what if …" He stopped as Stella turned her head to look at him. Her eyes were filled with hurt. He couldn't not believe her.

"Guys," Jamie called, returning to the living area from the bedroom.

"What's up?" Colin jumped.

"I called Tammy. She didn't answer, but I sent a text. She just replied. Said they got held up yesterday. They got lost and had some car problems, but they will be with us early this afternoon." Jamie's face was beaming.

The wave of relief that washed through the group was so strong it was almost a physical thing. Even Tony found himself thinking of things in a slightly different light.

"They're really coming?" Stella piped up.

"Yeah, Tammy said she would be on the way soon." The relief permeated deeper through their fear, and even Stella smiled.

"Well, it's almost daylight. Let's have some breakfast and see what happens," Colin suggested. "I'm starving."

There was not a lot of food in the fridge, but enough to whip up some bacon and pancakes. The meal turned out to be exactly what they needed.

Sitting together at the dining table, their mood lightened, and even Ricky once again joined in the conversation. The simple knowledge that they were in the right place made everything else that much more bearable.

"We should go for a walk or something," Colin suggested as he finished his pancakes and downed the last of his coffee.

"You mean like a hike?" Stella asked.

"Yeah, I mean, we know they are not going to be here until early afternoon. We can't sit around here all morning waiting for them." Colin looked at them.

"It might be good," Tony agreed, thinking about how they had only seen the place in the dark. "Going out during the day, it might, you know, put everything into perspective, help us get a clear look at the puzzle."

"Puzzle?" Stella asked, tilting her head.

"He means the whole thing from last night and this morning. It might help us piece together what happened," Jamie jumped in.

Tony smiled at his sister. She always had his back.

"Maybe, yeah. I mean, we were probably imagining things anyway," Stella said with false confidence. Tony felt it in her words, while the others seemed not to notice.

"Then it's settled. We'll tidy up and go for a hike. Doesn't have to be far, but at least we can go and do something outdoorsy." Jamie ended the discussion by standing up from the table and taking her dishes to the sink.

"There's no dishwasher," Ricky announced.

"Well, the last one back can do the dishes then," Jamie said with a smile, much to Ricky's obvious irritation. She hurried off into the bedroom, as one by one the others left the table and set about getting ready.

"I guess we're staying then," Stella said to Tony as soon as they were alone.

"You don't want to?" he asked.

"Do you?" She looked at him.

"We could just leave," Tony offered, knowing it was a crazy idea.

"No, we can't. They want to stay, so we will stay. We just have to hope that everything turns out for the best." Fear suffocated every word Stella spoke, and it was one that Tony felt and echoed in his thoughts.

"I'm sure it will all be fine," Tony said, giving her a friendly hug.

Stella's arm wrapped around him and pulled him close, their bodies pressed together. Stella didn't let go, and Tony, who normally struggled to get close to people, felt a strange calm wash over him at feeling Stella beside him.

CHAPTER SEVEN

Smoke hung in the air like a cloud, dampening the glow of the fluorescent light that flickered intermittently above their heads. The group, four strong, sat in a rough circle, waiting until the head of their group to arrive.

Two sat on chairs, while one sat on an overturned crate. The other, an obscenely large woman wearing an out-of-date floral summer dress, sat on an old oil can. She leaned back against the desk that sat in the back office of the garage. Sweat sheened her face, and no sooner had she raised her arm to wipe a tissue across her brow had the exertion caused the same amount to reappear.

They chatted nervously. A skinny man with long hair and big ears sat beside the woman, holding her hand, and stroking the back of her arm like a schoolboy in love. Across from them sat the large mechanic, who unclipped his overalls and scratched his belly while they waited, his flannel shirt barely containing the swollen abdomen. Beside him sat an older man, wiry and strong, with large glasses and a receding hairline that he tried to cover up with a bad combover.

"Would you look at these," the fat woman said, rummaging through the bag on the desk beside her. She pulled out a red lace bra and a matching thong. The material was tiny but looked even more so in her meaty fists.

Beside her, the man smiled, eyeing the underwear. He watched as the women brought them to her face and took a long sniff. "Clean ones too."

Her amorous fella was bouncing on his chair watching her, and looked utterly dismayed when she balled them up and threw them to the bespectacled man. "Here, Jim, I know you likes 'em too."

The man looked up and caught the underwear, giving a squeaked laugh before he shoved them down the front of his trousers. He didn't speak but groaned as his hand got to work rubbing the lace in all the right places.

"What you do that for, Mae? You'd look hot in them," the thin man complained.

"Don't worry, baby. Momma's got more of that good stuff, and tonight, you get to do whatever you want to me." Mae leaned over and near swallowed her man whole, their lips meeting in what could closest be described as a yawn as tongues noisily explored one another's mouths.

"Mae, Billy, cut it out. We've got business to attend to first," a strong voice spoke up, stopping the pair just as Billy's hand started to work its way over Mae's abundant thigh and up the bottom of her dress.

"Sorry, Gus," Billy replied, pulling his hand away.

The owner of the town grocery store walked in and took his seat at the head of their group. He didn't speak for a while, but instead, sat with his head lowered, as if in prayer.

"Did you deliver them packages, Hank?" he finally spoke.

"Sure did. Billy and I just got back," Hank, the town mechanic, answered.

"And their car?" Gus asked.

"Out back, under a tarp, ready to be stripped down and sold," Hank answered, pushing out his barrel chest.

"Good," Gus said, satisfied with the answer.

"They were close though," Billy said.

"Shut yer mouth, Billy," Hank snarled.

"What does he mean?" Gus looked from Hank to Billy and then back to Hank again.

"He don't mean nothing, Gus," Hank said, his words lacking any and all conviction.

The room was quiet for a second, while everybody sat waiting for the other to say something. Billy eventually obliged.

"Yes, I do. They were close. The mountain beasts. Like they were waiting for us. We hardly had time to tie 'em up before they came for dinner." There was genuine fear in Billy's words, but nobody could tell if it was fear of the beasts or of Hank's eventual retribution that was the most overpowering.

Gus listened and nodded. He pulled a cigarette out of the crumpled packet in his shirt pocket and lit it. His fingers had a tremor to them as he raised it to his lips and took a long drag.

"That true, Hank?" His words were calm, but his eyes were sharp and focused.

"Gus, it's not that simple. The girls, they were making a lot of noise. Probably called them down. We got things done in time and were away before they arrived," Hank answered, nervous. His eyes narrowed and sweat dripped from his nose.

The temperature in the room felt as if it had increased by ten degrees in the last thirty seconds.

"If they were close, then it means they were hungry. We need to keep them up in the mountains. We don't need them coming back down here again," Gus spoke with a hurried authority.

"Would they really come into town?" Mae asked, fanning herself with a used car manual.

"Done it before. Dang near wiped us out. My grandpa was one of the lucky few that made it. They tore right through us. Took four men to put one of them down. Their bodies are strong as if they wore armor plating. Bullets seemed to just bounce off them, so my grandpa always told me." Gus looked at Mae. "But con't you worry none. I've got us a plan to keep them happy."

Gus smiled, and Mae calmed. With that, the tension in the air dissipated, unlike the smoke cloud above them.

The four others sat and listened intently as Gus started to talk, allaying their fears using both the promise of a plan and the lessons learned from the previous battle with the beasts. He spoke with the skill of a master storyteller, regaling tales around a campfire, eager to pass on the legends to the younger generations.

"So those kids that came through earlier are all part of the same group?" Hank spoke once Gus was finished.

"Seems so. Lady luck was smiling on it. Now we got those first two. We've got the others up at Frank's old hunting cabin. All we got to do is bait them into staying longer, and we can bring the beasts down to them." Gus looked at them all. "It ain't nothing different than what we've done every time they get hungry. This is just a bigger meal, that's all."

"How do we keep 'em there? Want me and Billy here to pay them a visit?" Hank asked, a glint in his eyes.

"Not this time, Hank. We've got to play it smart. I have the girl's phone. Took it from that young bitch when she tried to bite me," Gus said, looking down at the wound on his hand. Susan had bitten through the skin between his thumb and forefinger, tearing away a deep gouge of flesh as she resisted his initial assault.

"You gonna call them, like in that scary movie we watched the other day?" Mae spoke, her hands clamped down on Billy's thighs, while she near salivated at the thought of terrorizing the kids at the cabin.

"No, these kids don't use phones for calling. They send these messages and such. We'll wait for morning, and then I'll drop them a message saying to wait until the afternoon," Gus said.

"Say car trouble. Always works, and I can give you a real good story," Hank pitched in, eager to play a part in the affair.

"That's good. I like it." Gus smiled. "So we know the drill. We need to feed these things again and fast. No time to have any fun with 'em. Sorry Hank, Billy ..."

"Billy's got enough fun coming his way tonight," Mae said as she tightened her grip on Billy's leg and pushed his hand up her dress.

Opposite them, Jim, Hank's brother, gave a growl as his hands stopped moving in his trousers. He whined like a scolded puppy, and his body went stiff. He slouched back in his chair, a spreading wetness around his crotch.

"Dammit, Jim, you made a mess. You need to wait for that sort of shit," Hank yelled, backhanding his brother across the face.

"Jimmy done cum in his pants," Mae said, laughing. "You're gonna have to shoot it into the real thing one day, Jimmy."

Mae's laughter filled the room, while Jim fell to the floor weeping.

"Leave him be, Mae. You know he can't help it." Anger flashed in Hank's face. Jim was his brother, and he would protect him until the end.

"Sorry, Hank, but I mean it, Jimmy. You need to feel what it's like to be inside a real pussy one day. Billy's tried it and now look at him. He's in love with it, ain't you, Billy." Mae's hand had reached Billy's crotch, and her grip at that moment in time was enough to get Billy to agree to pretty much anything.

"You gotta pick a good one though, Jim. Don't go grabbing any dry cunt. You want one that's big and wet," Billy said, his eyes crossing as Mae started to squeeze.

"Alright, that's enough. We have the plan, we'll take care of this together. No need for the others to find out about anything. We keep this to ourselves. Got it?" Gus looked around the room, and everybody nodded, apart from Jim, who was still lying on the floor crying.

With their meeting adjourned, Gus left the room quickly, while Hank helped his brother back to his feet.

Mae and Billy remained seated for a few moments, while Mae continued to tease her man before their mouths once again found their targets. Their noisy exchange of saliva irritated Hank, who cussed them out until they stopped.

"Get out of here, you two. If I have to see you fuck one more time, then I'm gonna feed both of you to the beasts."

The couple soon and left the garage and disappeared into the night.

"You be getting on home too, Jimmy. I've got to clean up here and everything. I'll be by in the morning to collect you," Hank instructed, shooing his brother out of the garage via that workshop doors. He pulled them closed and locked them, disappearing into the workshop to start taking apart the car.

CHAPTER EIGHT

It was just past nine when the group set off for their hike. Both Tony and Stella had tried to stall things, their minds bouncing back and forth between fearing what they thought they had seen to ridiculing themselves for allowing their active imaginations to get the better of them.

"Hey, slow down. We're not out for a run," Colin called out to Ricky, who had opened up a hefty lead on them.

He offered no answer and Colin was not inclined to call again. The others were clustered together, walking in a single line. Colin took the lead, with Jamie close behind, while Tony and Stella were a few paces further back.

The air was crisp but the sky was clear, and it didn't take long for them to realize that the surrounding trees created an environment that amplified both hot and cold conditions. This, coupled with the gentle but steady incline of the forest floor, made for a harder walk than they had anticipated.

Despite having moved ahead of them, the group caught up with Ricky in a small open patch of land. Tree stumps littered the clearing, with no sign of the fallen section of trees.

"Something tore them down," Stella whispered.

"Or they were rotten and fell during a storm," Ricky offered, the first thing he had said since the group left the cabin.

"It's just some fallen trees, guys. Come on. According to Google Maps, there's a really cool hiking trail not too far from here. We can make it and have lunch there, then follow it back toward the cabin," Jamie said, trying her hardest to please everybody.

"Or we could head that way," Ricky said, pointing to the right of where Jamie had indicated. "I looked around while I was waiting and there is some sort of old pathway. Not used much, but I bet it leads somewhere interesting."

The words were surprising, not just because of who spoke them, but because of the genuine tone with which they were uttered.

"I don't know. There's nothing marked on the map," Jamie said, hesitant.

"That's why it's an adventure. We wanted to check things out right, have a bit of fun. Well, where's your sense of adventure?" Ricky smiled. Being out in the open air held a positive effect on his mood and social skills.

"He's got a point," Colin said. "Didn't you tell me that you were looking forward to trying some new things and having a bit of fun?"

Jamie pouted but knew that Colin had a point. The old Jamie would have followed the safe path, gone the way of the masses. The new Jamie was a free spirit. *At least, she wanted to be,* she thought.

"Alright, but we keep an eye on the clocks. I don't want to get lost and miss Tammy arriving," Jamie said, throwing a glance over at her brother and Stella.

Neither offered any immediate objections and fell into line as they started walking again. Once again, Ricky's natural pace opened up a gap, but he seemed more observant to the fact and stopped frequently to let them catch up.

"Look there," Stella said, grabbing Tony by the arm.

She pointed through the trees at another felled tree. Only this time, the trunk had now been pulled away. It lay on the ground at an angle that looked unnatural for the position of the stump.

"There's something under it," Tony said, his eyes immediately drawn to the finer details of the scene.

"What is it? No, stay here," Stella said as Tony stepped away from the path and into the woods. "Wait for me."

Tony heard Stella and was relieved to feel her beside him, but part of his mind wished she had stayed where she was. He had a bad feeling bubbling in his stomach, and he didn't want to be responsible for her getting hurt.

The pair approached the felled tree, while ahead of them, the others had continued their journey; Ricky, lost in his thoughts, while Colin and Jamie chatted with one another, walking arm in arm when the path permitted.

Tony reached the trunk and crouched down. The wood was hard, and anything but rotten.

"This wasn't Mother Nature," he said, looking up at Stella. "Something knocked this thing down."

Stella had her arms crossed, hugging herself, and seemed to grow more pensive by the second. Tony stood, the notion to pull Stella into his arms flooding over him. He looked at her and thought he saw it in her eyes that she wanted him to do that same.

He couldn't though. Ricky was there, and he was behaving for the first time in two days. Tony turned away. His eyes scoured the tree trunk, looking for what had caught his eye from the path.

"Look at this." He bent down and after fishing around under the trunk for a moment, he stood, pulling a pair of scruffy shorts out from where they had been hidden.

"How did they get out here?" Stella asked, looking around nervously. "I want to go back to the cabin."

Tony walked over to her, and this time did wrap an arm around her. In response, Stella flung both arms around his waist and held him tight. "I'm sorry, but I just want to go back and wait for the others."

"Okay, we will go grab the rest and head back. We can have lunch at the cabin and we will be in time for Tammy to arrive."

"Okay," Stella agreed, turning to head back to the path.

"Hey guys, you coming to join us or what?" Colin's voice called through the trees. They had come to a stop further down the path and were looking back toward them, through the trees.

"Coming," Stella answered.

"Just cut through, it will be quicker. You're gonna want to see this," Jamie called back, her voice excited.

They cut to their right and headed through the trees. It was a clear shot to the others and cut a corner off the path. The ground all around them was stripped of any real foliage. The thick ferns and ground-level plants that filled the forest around the cabin were gone. None had noticed it as they walked, but standing there now, Tony realized how strange it was. A layer of leaves and general organic detritus created a blanket that covered the earth but further than that, it was just the trees.

Tony let Stella take a lead, keeping himself between her and the rest of the forest. He only stopped when he felt something snap beneath the weight of his foot.

"Jesus," he said, jumping.

"What is it?" Stella asked.

"Oh, it's nothing, just a dead bird, but I twisted my ankle trying to avoid it," Tony lied, as he quickly kicked some leaves over the yellowed bones where his foot had been.

"Poor thing," Stella said.

"I think it happened a while ago, probably never felt it coming," Tony said.

"I didn't mean the bird, silly," Stella said, looking up at him, their eyes locking.

Tony felt his heart shudder and his body tingle. He stopped dead in the woods, his feet turning to lead. He looked over at his sister and Colin, then back to Stella. She looked at him and smiled.

"Come on, they're waiting." She turned and carried on back to the group.

Tony looked back at the pile of leaves that he had created, covering the bones. He didn't want to take a second look at them because he was afraid that it would reveal exactly what he thought he saw. At least now, he could convince himself it was just a dead animal, a bird or rodent, and that was better than the truth any day of the week.

They made it through the trees and rejoined the others. The trail took a sharp turn, and Tony soon saw why. They had been steadily climbing ever since they left the cabin, and now found themselves on a ledge that ran across the mountains. The view was spectacular, looking out across the trees and the rolling landscape. The sun lit up the world, breathing life into so many different shades and colors. It looked like the sort of place someone would take a photograph that would become a postcard or some advertising image.

"Look down there," Jamie said, pointing down.

"Is that…?" Stella began.

"Yep, it's the town we came through yesterday," Colin answered before she could finish her question.

The town looked tiny below them, but at the same time revealed itself to be larger than they first thought. Several side streets branched off and off again, leading to homes and buildings of all sizes. They easily found the store and garage, but in the back, they spied a church and what looked to be an old-fashioned schoolhouse. There was a scrapheap too, on the edge of the town, the junk reflecting the sun as if trying to signal for their attention.

"It's strange that towns like this can exist still," Tony said, taking in the site, and the vast space around it. The miles and miles of empty country. "It's so isolated."

"We saw enough yesterday to prove that town is strange," Stella said, thinking back to the store and the weird man that ran it.

"When you live with such a limited and shared gene pool, you're going to go a little crazy," Colin said, his words sounding far more thoughtful than they were, or deserved to be.

"Guys, it's getting late, why don't we think about heading back?" Jamie said, checking her phone.

"Let's sit here, have some food, and then we'll turn around," Colin suggested.

Nobody had any objections.

"I need to take a leak," Ricky announced, wandering off into the trees before anybody could comment.

"He confuses me," Colin said, once the man was out of earshot. "He seems almost friendly today."

"He can be," Stella replied, lowering her head. "He just gets jealous and well, his temper can get the better of him."

"Has he ever hit you?" Tony asked.

"Tony," Jamie scolded him.

"Sorry," Tony replied, shrugging his shoulders at his sister. To him, it was a natural question to ask, but he assumed from her glare that it was a matter of his timing being wrong.

Stella wrapped her arms around herself and took a sandwich, ending the conversation. Tony looked up and saw Jamie scowling at him.

They ate in silence, the gentle wind rustling through the trees. Below them, the town looked tiny, almost like a toy, miniature village, left behind by some holidaying family with small children.

None of them noticed that Ricky never returned to the group, or that the sky had grown slowly darker while they ate, the clouds rolling in quickly over the hills, fat and pregnant with storm.

With the food eaten and the remains packed away, making sure that everything was collected, so as not to give any more bears an excuse to come following them, they got ready to head back.

"Hey, where's Ricky?" Jamie asked, looking around.

"He never came back, did he?" Colin looked at the others.

"Don't think so," Jamie replied.

"It's getting cold," Stella said, zipping up her thin jacket.

"And dark too," Tony added, looking out over the mountains. "It's going to rain, hard."

"Shit," Colin cursed. "Ricky, very funny, dude, now come on, we need to be heading back."

There was no answer, but the sound of something moving through the trees ahead of them got their attention.

"Ricky, enough games," Jamie shouted, her voice taking on the mothering tone it so often did when she was fed up.

Colin wasn't going to wait for an answer and so strode forward, his movements purposeful. Tony watched him and then looked around them. The darkness was creeping ever closer, and the trees were changing once again, the shadows and the shroud twisting into something sinister. He could feel it in the air and hear it in the silence that surrounded them.

"Let's just go," Tony suggested.

"Yeah, Colin, come on. Don't give him the satisfaction. Loser," Jamie snarled, turning to head back.

"Jesus Christ," Colin yelled suddenly as a deer sprang through the ferns and onto the path.

It stopped and eyed the group before bounding back into the trees, running full speed, dancing its way around the trunks and into the dark.

Before anybody could laugh at Colin, something rushed through the trees. The sound of cracking branches and heavy movements echoed around them. There was a scuffle and then silence again, as whatever was moving had stopped.

"I guess Mom caught up with Bambi and gave him a telling off," Colin said, trying to make light of the situation.

"Bambi's mom died," Tony said, stating the fact.

"Great analogy, guys. Let's go." Jamie took control, leading the group back the way they had come, as behind them, thunder rolled through the hills, bringing the storm closer and closer.

Their descent moved at a quicker pace, driven not only by an eagerness to get back to the cabin before the rain started but because they all felt it, the strange change that came over the hills when the sunlight fell. Nobody wanted to voice it, but Tony could see they all felt it this time.

They hurried in a group, not sticking to the single-line formation of earlier. There was safety in numbers. As such, they all came to a halt at the same time, the bloody carcass blocking the path getting their attention.

The deer's body was slick with blood, which still trickled from the stubby wound that had once been its neck.

"What the hell?" Jamie asked.

"Another bear attack?" Stella asked, looking over at Tony, whose face had paled considerably at the sight of so much blood.

A sudden movement to their left broke the spell that held them in place. Tony looked and saw something move through the trees. It was tall and walked like a man, but it disappeared before he could get a clearer picture of it. It was as if the forest opened up and absorbed it.

"Shit," Jamie said. She too was looking into the trees.

There was no real order given, but all four broke into a run, leaping over the deer, trying not to land or splatter too much in the bloody mud. Hurrying down the trail, they ran as fast as they could, the claps of thunder reverberating around them like the stampeding footsteps of whatever had been following them chasing them down.

"Don't stop," Jamie yelled as she ran, pulling ahead of the rest.

"Jamie!" Stella shrieked as a figure moved through the trees. It cut across the path between Jamie and the others.

"What the fuck was that?' Colin yelled as adrenaline surged through his body.

"It wasn't a bear, that's for sure," Tony offered, peering beyond the figure to where Jamie stood with her hands pressed against her mouth, as if trying to hold back the scream she had given.

"Where is it? Where did it go?" Stella asked.

The four were frozen to the spot, staring at the area of forest where the thing had disappeared.

"I don't see it," Colin said.

"We need to move," Tony offered, even though his own feet were rooted to the spot. He looked around, expecting to see the creature come charging through at them.

"Why is nobody moving?" Stella asked.

"Listen," Colin said, holding his hands out to hush the group. "I can hear it."

Footsteps, heavy, lolloping footsteps, but they were drowned out by the wind, which whipped up around them and made it sound as if the entire forest was coming alive and whispering to conspire against them.

Rain began to fall in fat, heavy drops, and as it grew heavier, the trees began to dance and sway in the shadows, creating the illusion of movement all around them. They were surrounded, and somewhere inside it all stood some mountain monster.

The fear that held them finally broke, and all four burst into a run, pushing themselves to the limit to race back to the cabin.

They tripped and stumbled, but they didn't stop. Colin twisted his ankle, but bit down on his lower lip and swallowed the pain, using it as fuel to drive his legs even faster. Branches whipped and tore at their skin. Tony's face stung by the time they broke into the clearing. The cabin loomed ahead of them.

Charging up the steps, they stood waiting as Colin fumbled for the keys, his hands trembling as he failed repeatedly to get the lock to turn. Finally, it clicked, and they spilled into the cabin, slamming the door behind them.

They all stood with their backs against the door, their heart rates thundering as if still trying to outrun whatever it was they had seen.

"That ... that thing," Jamie tried to speak.

"I told you," Tony said, breathlessly.

"It ... it couldn't have been," Colin offered, his mind not capable of voicing the full statement.

"We told you," Stella answered.

"Hey guys, what took you so long?" Ricky asked, his voice fresh and relaxed.

The four of them all looked up at him.

"What?" He saw their faces and heard the thunder rumble outside. "Oh shit, that storm moved in fast," he said, starting to turn away.

Colin moved first, striding towards Ricky, his fist already balled. "Where were you?" he snarled.

"I took a leak, got a little lost, and ended up back here," he answered, as if it was perfectly normal to ditch people in the woods.

"Oh, of course," Colin answered, his voice perfectly calm. It helped to keep Ricky off balance, so when Colin finally let his fist fly, it caught the man complete unaware.

The heavy thwack of the impact was painful to hear, and Ricky as good as melted into the floor, crumbling from the blow, which caught him right on the jaw.

"You insensitive asshole," Colin raged, his patience worn thin.

The others moved in, separating the pair, not that Ricky was in a position to offer much of a response from where he lay half-unconscious on the floor.

"You don't just fucking ditch people like that. It's not fucking safe here. We have to stick together," Colin ranted, unleashing his fear and frustrations in a curse-filled rant. He only stopped when Jamie put her hands on his shoulders and tried to lead him away, pushing him toward the kitchen area, hoping distance from Ricky would calm him down.

"Hey, hey, listen to me. It's going to be alright," Jamie soothed, unsure if she was talking the truth.

Colin looked into her eyes, the red mist clearing. He stood stiff, but after a few moments began to relax, and with a shuddering breath, he let go and the rage monster fell away.

"Shit," he said, bending over, resting with his hands on his knees as he gulped down several deep breaths. "I've never hit anybody before."

"Well, you do it pretty well," Jamie said, looking back to see Ricky sitting on the floor, his back against the sofa, his legs straight out before him. He was looking at Colin, but there was no anger in his eyes. It was a look of respect, and fear.

Tony and Stella looked after Ricky, who was spaced out for a good five or ten minutes after his altercation with Colin.

The fight seemed to have cleared the air a little between them all. Everything that had been underlining even the good mood of the morning was now gone, the natural order of things having been put in place. Colin was top dog, and Ricky understood this.

"We need to leave," Tony announced, once it was clear that a peace had been brokered.

"Leave? I think we are just starting to become friends," Ricky tried to joke.

"Didn't you see what was out there?" Jamie asked, shocked.

"There's nothing out there other than storm and trees," Ricky assured them.

"No, no, there's something else. Something living in the forest. It was—"

"Bigfoot," Stella said, finishing her friend's stammered sentence.

Ricky looked at them, his face twisted in disbelief. His face twitched, and it looked as if he was about to laugh. It never happened, however, because the large window in the kitchen area shattered, and the howl of the raging storm charged inside.

Only, it wasn't the storm that was howling. It was something else.

Stella screamed and pressed herself close to Tony. Ricky stared at the window, while Jamie turned and looked at what it was that had caused the damage.

The severed deer's head had continued to fly after it shattered the window and crashed into the wall. It bounced once before coming to a stop straight up, its dead eyes staring at the group, while tendrils of torn flesh fanned out around the stump of its neck like a bloody lace trim.

"Jesus Christ," Colin yelled, jumping backward, pulling Jamie with him.

Backpedaling, they rejoined the others and stood in a cluster, staring from the head to the window and back again.

"What...?" Ricky began to speak, but another crash caused the entire cabin to tremble. The kitchen wall gave a loud crunching, and the wooden beams splintered, creating a finger-wide crack in three of the panels.

Outside, the monster roared, and it felt as if the sky was falling in on them.

Tony watched everything unfold and felt his brain begin to cloud over. It was too much, too much to process and understand. The pieces of a thousand puzzles had been mixed together, and he was left trying to sort them out, in a race against the clock.

He felt Stella shudder beside him. Looking at her, he saw her pain, and the tears streaking her face. Suddenly, the puzzles no longer felt important. He needed to protect her. They needed to escape.

Looking around the room, Tony saw it for what it was: A wooden box, a mausoleum that would hold their bones until the creatures that hunted them ground them to dust.

Then his eyes fell on them, mounted on the wall above the fireplace, a piece of decoration so stereotypical for the setting that they had never questioned or noticed them before.

"Guys, there," he said, pointing to the two hunting rifles that were mounted to form a cross.

Colin reacted first, running to the wall and yanking them both free as another blow was dealt to the cabin, from the other side now, shattering the window behind them.

A face appeared, black and feral, the yellow eyes glowing like those of a demon patrolling its own patch of hellground.

Everybody screamed as the beast opened its mouth and gave a roar that sounded like a jet engine preparing to take flight.

Colin raised one of the rifles, took quick aim, and pulled the trigger. It clicked empty.

"They're not loaded," Colin said, as he brought them back to the group.

"I saw some shells in the kitchen," Ricky offered, hurrying away.

The creature in the window stood to full height, its chest filling the hole it had created. Another clubbing blow shook the house and made the ceiling lamps dance, swinging to and fro like lanterns on a ship caught in a storm.

Ricky returned with a box of shells and threw a couple at Colin who caught them, and without a moment's hesitation, threw the second rifle back at Ricky in return.

Jamming the rounds into the rifle's chamber, Colin took aim at the massive chest and fired. Unable to miss such a massive target, the rounds buried themselves in the muscle, yet the two streams of red that flowed from the wounds only seemed to further infuriate the beast.

"How many are there?" Ricky asked as he chambered rounds in his weapon and turned to look at the kitchen window.

"I don't know. We only saw one," Tony answered, looking around him in all directions.

"Well, there's sure more than that now," Ricky answered, firing a shot at something as it moved past the kitchen window.

The cabin took another blow in return and the wood splintered further. One more shot and the wall would cave in.

"We need to get out of here," Jamie screamed. "The car."

"We'll never get there before they tear us apart," Colin said as he slid two more rounds into his weapon.

"Why are they doing this?" Stella cried as she clung desperately to Tony, who held her close against him.

There was no time to answer because an almighty crash saw the damaged section of wall burst inwards, the wood splintering. Chunks of wood flew in all directions, flung by the force of the impact and the ferocity of the storm. Wind and rain swirled through, creating a cloud of debris which slowly cleared to reveal a Bigfoot standing in the hole it had created.

The creature was taller than all of them, at least seven feet, its frame thick and heavy with muscle, buried behind long, matted fur. A rotten stench swirled on the wind, and for a moment, the group squared off with the beast.

Its eyes studied them, nostrils twitching as it committed their odor to memory.

"Get down," Colin called, as he fired the rifle through the others.

The first round caught the creature in the shoulder, knocking it backward, but the heavy coat limited the damage that was done.

Taking the lead offered by Colin, Ricky raised his rifle and fired two rounds, both of which embedded themselves in the creature's torso. Enraged, the beast gave a roar and lunged towards them, closing the gap in a single stride. Its long arms swung out, missing the group who turned and fled deeper into the cabin.

Steadying himself, Colin fire one last round, which tore through the side of the Bigfoot's skull, ripping the ear and a chunk of flesh free, peeling it away down to the bone.

Stunned, the creature stopped, pain registering on its face before another blast put it on the floor. The round tore a fist-sized chunk from the creature's neck, which caused its head to hang at a strange angle. Blood and gristle misted the air, spraying both Jamie and Tony, who himself had moved in front of Stella the moment the wall collapsed. He had armed himself with a fire iron and wielded it like a broadsword.

The Bigfoot dropped not unlike a man, first falling to its knees before it pitched forward, its heavy body landing with a resolute thud.

"Is it dead?" Colin asked, as he spun around, training his weapon on the other side of the building, where he was certain at least one more creature stood.

Ricky didn't answer straight away but prodded the beast with his foot. The immense weight of the frame meant it didn't budge.

"It smells dead," Jamie said as she wiped the gore from her face.

Ricky reloaded his rifle and pressed the barrel against the Bigfoot's head. He stared at it for a moment before pulling the trigger. From such close range, the skull cracked open like an egg, leaking brain and blood through the crack.

A crash from the rear of the cabin told them that the fight was far from over. The howls of the however many Bigfoot that still surrounded the cabin created a wave of noise that threatened to deafen them, rumbling with enough force to shake their bones and organs.

Behind them, the living room window shattered, peppering them with slivers of glass that lacerated their flesh like hungry teeth.

"We're surrounded," Stella screamed as Colin's hunting rifle boomed, missing the target but decimating the remnants of the window frame.

The creature ducked back out of sight, but before they could rest, another crash came from the bedroom.

"They're inside," Ricky called as he shouldered his rifle.

"I'm out. How many rounds you got left?" Colin called, backing up half a step in preparation for whatever came from the bedroom.

He never saw the shaggy arms come through the window, and the entire property held the stench of Bigfoot, which made it impossible for him to tell one creature from the other.

The first thing Colin knew about being taken was as the hand closed around his skull, he managed to begin a scream but never gave it full voice. The strong hand squeezed and crushed his skull like it was a piece of rotten fruit. Blood and brains oozed through the creature's grip, while an eyeball shot through the air like a party popper, hitting the turning Jamie in the forehead before dropping to the floor at her feet.

Jamie screamed.

Colin caught his sister as she collapsed, just as the wall between the master bedroom and living area burst apart. It was as if someone had let off a grenade. A shower of splinters flew through the air, peppering Ricky like arrows fired at Gulliver when he first arrived in Lilliputia.

"We need to get out of here," Ricky yelled as he ran over to them.

He narrowly missed being decapitated by the door that was hurled in his direction by a large and clearly female Bigfoot. Her jet-black fur did nothing to hide the large breasts that covered her chest. Despite their size, they were an equally effective armor compared to that of her male counterparts. The wound that Ricky inflicted had not even caused her to break stride as she marched into the house.

"We need to get to the car," Jamie said, as the other Bigfoot pulled Colin's body out of the house via the smashed living room window.

"We'll never reach it," Ricky said. "I've only got two rounds left."

"You can drive right?" Tony spoke, taking a purposeful step towards Ricky.

"Fuck yeah, I can drive," Ricky replied.

"Great, because I can't." Tony grabbed the gun, acting on instinct, ignoring the multitude of puzzle pieces that lay shattered in his mind. Adrenaline drove him, an animal sense of survival. He yanked the gun out of Ricky's hands. "Get them out of here."

Without another word, Tony turned and ran out of the house, disappearing into the storm, hooting and hollering at the Bigfoot in an attempt to pull them away from the house.

"Tony!" both Stella and Jamie screamed, but it was too late. Tony was gone.

"You heard him, ladies. Get to the car," Ricky said, grabbing the pair, his asshole personality not completely destroyed by the horrifying turn of events.

Using more force than was necessary, Ricky shoved the girls out of the door and down to the car, which sat where they had parked it, albeit in a far worse state than when they had arrived.

"Shit, what do we do?" Stella screamed when she saw the battered vehicle.

"Get in, shut up, and hope it fucking drives." Ricky gave her a final shove toward the wreck of Colin's car.

They forced open the rear and driver's door and piled inside. Soaked to the skin by the pelting rain, but somewhat cleansed of the blood that had covered them, Ricky fumbled for the spare key which was tucked into the sun visor. The Bigfoot was nowhere to be seen, having fallen for Tony's diversion, but Ricky had no plan to wait around and confirm just how successful it was.

"Hold on," he said as he forced the gearbox into reverse.

CHAPTER NINE

"Where's Tony?" Jamie screamed as the car backed away from the cabin. The building was in ruins, two walls completely gone, and the Bigfoot standing on the roof looked on the verge of breaking through.

"He ran into the trees," Ricky answered as he saw two of the beasts stop just in front of the reversing car.

Their yellow eyes stared at them with pure fury. To the right, a rifle blasted, hitting the right-sided Bigfoot in the shoulder, getting their attention.

"There, I see him," Stella says, her eyes peering into the trees.

"You have to stop," Jamie pleaded, but Ricky wasn't listening.

The two Bigfoot took off into the woods, and Ricky used the chance to hit the handbrake and twist the crumpled car around so that they were driving forward. The windshield was cracked, a spiderweb pattern that ran across the entire surface, but he could see enough to drive still.

"Stop," Jamie screamed again, but Ricky planted his foot on the gas and the car took off.

The road away from the cabin was not as straight as they remembered, and soon, they were twisting and turning their way through the trees, with the shadows of Bigfoot chasing them down.

The sky flashed with lightning and a figure darted out from the trees.

Ricky swerved, not wanting to hit any Bigfoot. Colliding with their massive bodies would be like driving head first into a concrete pillar.

"Wait," Stella screamed. "Wait, that was Tony."

Ricky looked at her in the rearview mirror, his eyes burning with jealousy.

"Please stop," Jamie asked, her voice broken with grief.

Ricky never broke his glare with Stella but took his foot off the gas. "I won't stop, but he can jump in."

"Thank you," Jamie said as she kicked open the battered passenger door. "Tony, jump in."

Tony was running after the car, his rifle abandoned. They couldn't see any Bigfoot, but that didn't mean they were going to stop and check. Ricky brought the car to little more than a crawl as Tony drew closer to them.

His put his foot on the gas the instant Tony had hold of the frame, giving him barely enough time to hurl his body through the door. Jamie was on hand and grabbed his shoulders, hauling him into the car as they sped away, the door slamming shut as they picked up speed.

"Where are we going?" Stella asked, shouting to be heard over the thundering of her heart.

"What about Tammy?" Jamie's voice was distant as if she had no idea the words were coming from her mouth.

"Don't know, don't care. Call me an asshole, but I'm getting out of here," Ricky said with a snarl, his fists gripping the wheel with white-knuckled intensity.

"I agree with him. Let's head to the town. Safety in numbers," Tony panted, out of breath and running out of adrenaline to keep him pumped.

The Bigfoot were everywhere, running through the trees, keeping up with the car as it tried to follow the path. They hurled rocks and branches at them, peppering the car's body like insurgents attacking a convoy.

"Watch out," Stella screamed as a boulder the size of a Labrador crashed against the front of the car, crushing the metal with the same crisp sound of a can being trodden underfoot.

The warning came too late to avoid the collision, but Ricky managed to keep the car on the road and moving forward. The crushing impact took out the remaining headlight and plunged the group into darkness. The wipers could barely cope with the onslaught of rain, and a howling war cry carried on the breaths of the storm.

The Bigfoot could smell victory.

"Oh my God, we're going to die," Jamie said, clinging to her brother's arm as if it could somehow hold the reaper at bay.

"Wait, wait, listen," Tony said.

"Listen to what?" Stella asked.

"They're gone. Can't you hear it?" Tony looked at his sister, Stella, and even at Ricky.

"All I hear is the storm and this fucking motor complaining about doing its damned job," Ricky growled.

Tony sat back and closed his eyes. His head ached from all the noise and input. The darkness of his own creation was a quieter place and allowed him to focus his thoughts and clear his mind. He quickly yet methodically worked at the mountain of puzzle pieces that were strewn everywhere; not making the puzzles themselves but sorting everything into the right pile. Many were missing, all from the same pile. He was sure of it.

He opened his eyes.

"It's okay. They are gone," he said with certainty.

Ricky slowed the car down, hoping the drop in speed would calm the angry engine. "Fuck me, I think he's right." He peered through the smashed windscreen, squinting like a man without his glasses. The night was total around them, but nothing was being thrown at the car, and the yellow eyes of the Bigfoot no longer seemed to be chasing them down.

"That's great, but keep going. We need to get to the town," Jamie spoke, her voice growing stronger. "There are people there. They can help us. They have to."

"Yeah, well, it looks like things aren't all going to go our way tonight." Ricky thumped his hand against the steering wheel, as the car gave an angry growl before it cut out and went silent.

They crawled to a halt and sat there. Surrounded by storm, the night closed in around them, creating a claustrophobic atmosphere of death.

Panic rode on the wings of darkness, flung down from the heavens, riding each lightning bolt, and sent tumbling to the ground by every thunderous rumble that followed it up.

"We're going to do…what are we going to do?" Jamie asked.

"Well, we can either sit like sardines in a can and wait for those things to come and eat us, or we get moving and hustle it down to the town. It can't be far from here now." Ricky clearly had no intentions of waiting for either discussion or agreement, for his door was open before he finished speaking.

"He's right," Stella said, sounding almost disappointed to admit it.

"They are still out there. They killed Colin. I… I don't want to die." Jamie dissolved into a mess of tears and snot, finding comfort in the arms of the brother she had spent her life trying to protect.

"They are gone. There's no puzzle pieces for them anymore," Tony whispered, the puzzle pieces part of a dialogue the two of them shared.

"Are you sure?"

"I'm positive."

The words had the desired effect on Jamie, for she relaxed and dried her eyes with the back of her sleeve. She looked at her brother and her best friend. "Let's go."

Together, they got out of the car and stepped into the storm.

The rain slashed at them as if pelting shards of glass, while the wind howled through the trees. In the darkness, it was as if they had landed in some alien world. Nothing was familiar to them. Everything posed a threat, and death lived in the shadows around them.

"Which way?" Stella shouted above the wind.

Tony pointed down the road, which was illuminated by a streak of lightning overhead. It connected with a tree not so far from them, and they could hear the bark crack from the charge.

Soaked to the skin, and with their feet sinking ankle deep into the mud, they made the trek down. Slow going and exhausted, they expected the Bigfoot to swarm on them at any second.

It was Stella that first spied the light in the window, pointing it out to the others. The relief that swept through them created an energy that drove them on. Even Ricky, who they had caught up with along the way, seemed to feed off the vibe.

"I think the rain is letting up too," Stella said as she stood looking at the house.

"Let's see if someone is home." Ricky smiled as he walked to the front door.

There was no clear sign of a bell, so Ricky balled his fist and rapped on the door. It wiggled loosely in the frame. They waited, but there was no answer. Ricky knocked again, a hammer fist approach that had to be heard.

"There's light around here," Stella said, moving along a wall and around the corner to the long side of the building.

She couched down and peer carefully through the glass. It was dirty and cracked, but she could still see clear enough to wish that her eyes had been clawed out by one of the beasts they were fleeing.

She spun around to face the others, her expression enough of a warning to elicit concern from the rest.

"What is it?" Jamie asked, reaching out to steady her friend.

Ricky and Tony moved toward the window and peered inside, their stomachs equally turned by what they saw.

A skinny man, whose bones could be counted as he moved against the sofa, a gimp mask over his head, furiously fucked the enormous behind of an obese woman who lay bent over the sofa. Her bulk was so considerable that the far end of the piece of furniture was raised into the air and fell back against the floorboards with each thrust.

Her white skin was stained red with palm strikes, and as they watched, the man slapped her flesh and dug his fingers deep into the doughy mass. The woman turned her head toward them, and they flinched, but needn't have worried. She was blindfolded and had an apple stuffed into her mouth, like a suckling pig at a medieval feast.

"I'm going to be sick," Jamie said as she too peeked through the glass, against the advisement of the other three members of her group.

"The town is right there, let's keep going," Tony said, pointing further down the road. "The storm is letting up, and those two ... those two don't need us."

"Those two are what is wrong with this town." Stella shuddered as she remembered the encounter in the shop on their way through the day before. "They're probably related." She stepped back from the house, as if whatever secrets it harbored were catching.

They backtracked from the building and followed the road back down. They went around one corner and they stood on the border of the town. The paved road began and the stoplight where they had raced the tractor the day before flashed a constant amber at them. Like a lighthouse guiding ships in a storm, it gave them a reference point. The garage was close by. They would have a phone and a car. Maybe they could buy a car and get going before the Bigfoot came back to finish the job they started.

The town looked deserted, and while the darkness of the storm made it feel as if they were creeping around in the middle of the night, the truth was it was barely mid-afternoon. Even in a storm, there should have been more activity.

"Let's head to the garage," Ricky suggested.

"No," Stella shrieked, as the memory of the fat man's whispered words caressed her flesh and chilled her worse than any storm ever could.

"It's our best shot. The guy might be able to fix the car, or at least sell us one." Ricky had decided, and that meant the group would follow.

None liked it, but his alpha male personality was what they needed.

Ricky led the way, with Jamie following him. Tony walked with Stella, her arm around his waist.

"It's going to be alright," Tony spoke softly.

"How can you be so sure?" Stella looked up at him, her face paled by the rain, her tanned skin and dark hair seeming to shimmer in the rain, while her hazel eyes were wide and brimming with fear.

"Because I promise I won't let anything happen to you." Tony smiled and put his arm around Stella's shoulders.

It was an act of closeness that he was not often comfortable with, yet with her beside him, it felt like the most natural thing in the world.

CHAPTER TEN

They hurried along the street, flinching at each clap of thunder, constantly checking over their shoulders. Each time there was nothing, but their fear never faded.

The garage looked closed, except for the one light in the office. Even then, it looked dim, seeping through the faded curtains like something lecherous.

The workshop door was open, and it offered a shelter from the rain that was too great to resist. Huddling just over the threshold, afraid of venturing too far and incurring the wrath of the owner, they looked around. There was a car not too far from them, hidden under a sheet, protecting it from the rain and the general dirt and grime of the workshop.

"I bet whatever under there is something special," Ricky said, pointing at the vehicle. "We could take it, get the fuck out of this backwater town."

"No, we can't. It's not ours." Jamie stepped back, as if recoiling from the concept. Then she thought about it. She had promised Colin she would stop being the old Jamie. She would take more risks and have more adventures. Stealing a car was exactly what the new Jamie would do.

"You think these assholes will help us? Look around; there's nobody here." Ricky swept his arms around to indicate the vast emptiness of the garage.

"We can drive to the police, report the Bigfoot and the bodies. Maybe they can call the National Guard or something," Stella chimed in.

Ricky grabbed the sheet, and without waiting for any further agreement from the group, pulled it away revealing car underneath.

"No, No, it can't be." Jamie clasped her hands to her face and repeated her denial over and over, not even stopping when Tony tried to comfort her.

"What's wrong?" Stella asked.

"Shut the fuck up, you stupid bitch," Ricky snarled, his eyes sharp with anger, his cheeks puffed with held breath, and his fists clenched.

Tony didn't need to take long to put that puzzle together. Ricky was about to snap.

"Jamie, Jamie, calm down. Remember the house; remember our space in the attic. You told me I was safe there, that the busyness of the world couldn't find me. Go there now." Tony pulled all the tricks his sister had used on him over the years.

The attic had become his refuge, hiding away with all the long-forgotten memories and family secrets.

"It's ... that's ... the car. It's Tammy's car." Jamie turned to run, desperate to escape the realization that was slowly starting to dawn on them.

She didn't get far. The store owner was standing in the opening, pelted by rain, his jacket glistening wet, making him look like a monster from a horror movie shown late at night on cable television.

"What are you doing here?" he asked, his voice inquisitive yet laced with an underlying fear that he would never show.

Jamie tried to back away, but his arms moved fast and grabbed her by both wrists.

"Let her go." Tony began to move forward but behind him, Ricky gave a cry.

Tony turned.

Stella screamed.

Ricky collapsed.

A pool of blood already forming around him. The fat man from the store stood by the car, a tire iron in his hands, and a grin on his face that told them exactly how much trouble they were in.

"Leaving so soon?" he said, a sneer on his face.

The fat man took a step over Ricky's unconscious body and Tony flinched, moving to put himself between Stella and the man that was eyeing her the way a cat eyes a bird on the lawn.

"Out my way, boy." The tire iron moved fast and caught Tony in the gut, doubling him over.

"Tony!" Jamie screamed, but a backhand from the store owner silenced her, knocking her to the floor.

Tony gasped for breath, aware that Stella was still behind him. He tried to stand, pushing away the fire that raged in his belly, but a blow to the back of the head sent him hurtling to the floor. He sank deeper into the oil-stained concrete, sinking further and further until the darkness encompassed him completely. The last thing he remembered was Stella screaming, and a sudden surging will to rise back to the surface, but the force exerted on him was too much, and he fell back down into darkness's soothing embrace.

Stella watched Tony fall to the floor and felt her hopes of surviving slide down with him. The fat mechanic advanced on her, his smile stretched long and thin over his bloated face, sweat already glistening from the exertion of a few swings of the tire iron.

He grabbed her, tearing open her shirt, his eyes widening like a boy getting his first peek at a little bit of skin.

"Hank, you don't touch her now. We need her for them," the store owner growled. He had picked Jamie up from the floor and held her roughly by the elbows.

"I wasn't going to hurt her none, Gus. But don't you remember what she bought in your store?" Hank said, staring at his friend.

"Aye, I do. Good thinking, Hank." Gus understood what Hank was suggesting. "What about you, Missy? Are your cycles aligned?"

Gus laughed as he pushed his hands down Jamie's trousers. Jamie screamed and bucked against him, snapping her jaws as if she intended to tear his throat apart with her teeth.

"Nope, she's dry as a bone." The statement seemed highly entertaining to both men. They wasted several moments lost to laughter, and had their captives not been so exhausted, they may well have tried an attempt at escape.

Hank ripped off Stella's shirt while Gus grabbed some rope and tied Jamie's arms behind her back.

"They are gonna smell you a mile away, pretty thing," Hank said as he worked, removing Stella's trousers and binding her in a similar fashion to Jamie as he worked.

The two girls were pushed together, and with arms behind their backs and their ankles bound together, they were forced down onto the floor.

"You sit right there, while we decide what to do with you," Gus said, smirking. "Hank, go get the others; we need a meeting."

Hank left, and Gus got busy securing Tony, making sure that girls could see what he was doing. The garage seemed a lot smaller than it had when they arrived. Everything closed in around them. The storm outside was almost over, the rain reduced to little more than a drizzle, yet there was something beneath the distant rumbles of thunder. Something ferocious, and it was coming for them. The real storm had yet to begin, but when it hit, nobody would be safe.

CHAPTER ELEVEN

Ricky came to with a heavy feeling in his head. His body felt numb, the way his leg would do if he sat in one position for too long. His lips were swollen, and his tongue felt strange in his mouth.

He tried to move, but pain flooded through him, lighting up his vision with bursts of white light that blinded him and made him flinch, inspiring yet more pain to surge through his body.

His brain felt scrambled, and as he tried to piece together the events that led to his waking, the realization that alcohol had not been involved began to come to the forefront.

He remembered blood, lots of blood; the creatures in the woods and the attack on the cabin. His heart began to beat faster and faster. A tidal wave of adrenaline coursed through his body, washing away the pain, clearing his head.

He tried to move but realized his face was stuck to the floor. Panic crept in. Ricky closed his eyes and tried again. Whatever held him gave and he rose to his knees. The first thing he saw was blood, his blood. A pool of it had gathered around his body, staining his clothes and his flesh. Gingerly, he reached up and felt the egg-sized lump on the back of his head and the deep gash that ran along it.

"Come on, boy, don't fight me on this." The words made him freeze. He was not alone.

Turning slowly, he saw a man wrestling with another body. He recognized it as Tony, the half-retarded prick that stole his girl.

He could hear the girls' muffled cries too, but they were unimportant. He needed to escape.

Fuck them for turning on him. Fuck her for ruining the weekend. *The cunts almost got you killed. Leave them to what they deserve* he thought as he tried to take full control of his body.

He saw the shadow of the car beside him and started to crawl, inching his aching body around it, hoping he could hide before the fat man noticed he was moving.

Crawling on his hands and knees, like a drunk on the final leg of an epic journey home, Ricky made it to safety. His plan was to steal the car and escape. That ended when he saw the car had been stripped of its wheels. He hadn't noticed it before. His heart sank.

Looking around, he saw nothing else inside the garage that could offer him any escape. Trying hard to keep his breathing slow, and his inhalations quiet, Ricky forced himself to look further. The sky was clearing and the afternoon light was starting to rise, like a second dawn, offering him a new chance. His eyes saw the truck, and he knew it was his only chance.

He would have to run and move by the girls too, but if he made it, he would be free.

Peering through the car windows, he saw the older man was almost done stringing Tony up. He had to move now.

He tested his legs. They seemed to work fine. It was just his head and the incessant pounding of the wound. His vision blurred in time with the thunderous beating of his heart, but it didn't matter.

Ricky took three big breaths and forced himself to his feet. He set off, his pace less a run and more a speedy lollop. He felt like a zombie, his body sluggish and unwilling to truly listen to the commands he was giving it.

He heard the girls gasp as they saw him rise, but he ignored them, not even sparing a glance in their direction. His eyes were focused on the truck.

"Hey, you, stop there." The older man had seen him. He needed to move faster.

Willing his legs to run, they responded with a burst of speed that brought him to the rear of the truck. More voices greeted him. He looked around and saw a fat man advancing on him, with two more figures following behind him.

He tripped and stumbled but didn't fall. Holding onto the side of the vehicle, he pulled himself along and into the driver's seat. Ricky fumbled for the keys as his vision began to dim. His hands were tacky with blood, and he could feel the fresh stream running down his neck.

The keys were in the ignition, and the truck caught at the first attempt. His foot found the gas just as a hand grabbed him, yanking hard to try and wrench him from the driving seat. The truck took off, lurching forward as Ricky half-fell from the vehicle. The sudden movement of the truck caused the fat man to let go and after a mad scramble, Ricky hauled himself back behind the wheel and was gone.

The truck crashed into the three parked cars as it tried to right itself on the road and sped into the night.

The group of men, led by the panting mechanic, watched it drive away, heading out of town and back up into the forest.

Stella had felt a glimmer of hope well up inside her when she saw Ricky begin to stir behind the man they called Gus, as he wrestled with Tony. She was worried Tony was dead because he had not yet moved after the blow to the back of his head.

She had kept quiet, but when Ricky stood on the other side of the car, she had lost it. Jamie saw him too and screamed into the gag that covered her mouth.

Ricky hadn't even looked at them. He had not looked at her. As she heard the shouts outside, and the angry revving of a car engine, she knew he had left them. She heard the truck pull away and her heart shattered into a million pieces. She had never really loved Ricky, but he had made her feel good. Worthless too, at times, but mostly good, when they were alone. He had left them, and he had left her behind and now they were going to die.

Stella lowered her head and wept, watching as her tears streaked her bare flesh and dripped onto the cold concrete beneath them.

Ricky fought to control the vehicle. He knew he hit things, but he didn't care what. He just needed to put distance between him and them. The fucking hillbillies could have the others, but they wouldn't get him.

By the time he realized where he was going, the truck was moving too fast. He swerved from one side of the road to the other, his foot on the gas, and his brain no longer making the right connections to move it anywhere else.

His right-hand side felt numb. His arm was cold, and it felt as if he had been lying in the snow. It wouldn't respond or turn the wheel. Without warning, it fell into his lap and his whole body tipped over toward the passenger seat. The car veered from the road and crashed into a tree coming to a thumping halt, throwing Ricky forward into the center console. His body twisted and condensed from the impact, and he felt his ribs snap. He wasn't sure how many but knew from the way he could no longer breathe that the damage was not good.

Kicking out weakly, Ricky managed to force open the jammed door of the truck and slid out to the ground like a snake. He sat on the soaked earth, his back against the truck, his blood mingling with the mud. Unable to catch his breath, unable to move his right arm, he pressed his head back against the truck and began to weep.

He smelled them before he saw them. The overpowering stench made the hairs on the back of his neck and on his arms stand on end. They began to ache, as if the odor was so foul it could burn them away. Ricky stared at the trees and saw the shapes standing there, hidden by the shadows, but being slowly revealed by the passing storm, their giant bodies thick with muscle, eyes gleaming. One strode forward, appearing from the trees with lips pulled back to reveal long fangs, stained from years of dealing death with its jaws.

"I'm sorry," Ricky managed to proclaim to whoever was listening before the Bigfoot grabbed him by the ankles and hauled him into the air.

Suspended, the blood rushing to his head, Ricky vomited and passed out, throwing himself at the approaching blackness so that he wouldn't have to be part of his own demise.

Irritated by the man's ugly expulsion, the Bigfoot snarled and whipped Ricky's body against the truck with enough force to lift it up onto its side. Ricky's spine snapped with an audible pop, like a twig snapping underfoot. He landed face down in the mud, unable to move, unable to scream, but fully conscious of the fact that he was drowning.

The Bigfoot gave a growl and looked around at the others of its kind. Without a sound or any attempt at communication, they started off once more and continued their war march.

CHAPTER TWELVE

Pain brought Tony back into the conscious world, a burning, tearing heat that started in his shoulders and traveled through his arms before shooting out of his fingertips like magic. His head hurt, and everything was a jumble. Fragments of memories and what was going on all mixed together, as if somebody had taken all the puzzles in the world and thrown them together on the floor, kicking the pieces around for extra measure.

As he raised his head and opened his eyes, it was like a curtain being raised at the theater, revealing the set that had been so lovingly constructed behind the scenes. Tony looked around, taking in his surroundings. They were inside, and it was not the cabin. He remembered the Bigfoot and their escape.

The garage.

They were in the garage.

There was a car, and they were planning on escaping with it.

The others were gone. No, not gone, just not with him. They would never leave him behind. Ricky maybe.

Ricky was Stella's boyfriend.

Jamie would never let them leave. Neither would Stella.

Piece by piece, Tony sorted everything and began to construct the image of where they were.

He tried to move but couldn't. His feet barely touched the floor, and the fire raging in his arms and shoulders only got worse when he moved. Tony struggled and realized his arms were stuck, tied and bound behind his back. Then he remembered the mechanic. He had hit Ricky and then hit him.

Panic surged through him, and Tony was unable to hold it at bay. The understanding that the people in the town were not going to help them was overpowering. His mouth is covered with something, and the scent of oil and grease was strong. The rag in his mouth was dirty, and Tony wanted to spit it out. He tried and gave a frustrated growl when nothing worked the way he was used to or needed it to.

Looking up, Tony saw that he was not only restrained, but also tied up to the base of the car lift, which had been extended, not to its full height, but enough to keep Tony at bay and out of trouble. As his eyes scanned the room, desperate for something that could be interpreted as hope, he found it in a pair of deep hazel eyes. They stared at him from across the garage. Soft yet defiant, they held his gaze, and the relief at seeing them helped calm the torrid storm in his mind and gave him focus. The puzzle pieces seemed less intense, less important somehow.

Beside Stella, Tony saw his sister. She was sitting on the floor, hunched up, her knees drawn to her chest, her head lowered. She was scared. Unlike Stella, who had been stripped to her underwear, Jamie was fully clothed. Tony wanted to call out to them, but the gag in his mouth prevented it, and something else stopped him too; a piece of the puzzle he had overlooked but at the same time knew all along. They were not alone. The mechanic who had tied them up was still there. He had to be.

There was a room to the girls' right, Tony's left. The door was not fully closed. Tony could hear voices coming from the other side, even though he had no idea what they were saying.

Another burst of pain brought his mind back. He couldn't help anybody while he was tied up. They needed to escape. He had to find a way out.

Tony took another look at Stella. Her eyes were staring at him, and he held her gaze. He watched as she slowly flicked her head as if trying to shake away a fly or a stray hair. It took several seconds for Tony to understand what she was doing. He looked to his right, following the direction of Stella's head movements.

He saw the control box for the car lift hanging a few feet away from him. He couldn't reach it, not from where he was. Looking up, tears brought on by the pain in his arms, blinding him, Tony put everything together. He was tied with a rope; a crude but effective knot. He needed to move himself over to the controls. Already standing on his toes, he wouldn't make it, not without swinging himself.

Tony looked around. They were still alone in the workplace. He reasoned he only had one chance because if the box fell to the floor, it would alert the others and most likely fall beyond his reach.

Closing his eyes, Tony took several slow breaths and thought about the attic, the place his sister had taken him to when they were children, the place she had made his with her safe words and caring mind. When he opened his eyes again, Tony was ready and started to sway himself back and forth, his eyes set firmly on the control box.

Stella watched as Tony swung his body back and forth, running on his toes for a few steps before he needed to push off. Each swing brought him a little closer, but the pain etched into his face was clear. It rolled from his head in every bead of sweat. Agony overflowed from his being and for several minutes, it looked as though he wouldn't make it.

Stella bit down onto the rag in her mouth. She tasted oil and the warm copper flavor of fresh blood but didn't care. She bit down to keep the screams locked inside. Beside her, Jamie sat, unmoving. If it wasn't for the shuddering inhalations she made, Stella would have thought her friend was dead.

She knew the others were still in the garage somewhere: The mechanic and the store owner, Hank and Gus; two men who made her quiver at the mere thought of their names. She also knew that Ricky was gone. He had abandoned them, left them behind to die. She cried bitter, angry tears.

Tony inched his way ever closer and was swinging in a large arc, only touching the ground to push himself off to close that distance between him and their last hope at salvation. While he was suspended, his entire body weight was placed on his bound arms. He grimaced, but never slowed, and never looked to stop.

She gasped as his body twisted and his fingers brushed the device, shaking it loose, almost sending it tumbling to the floor. The true depth of her alarm was dampened by the gag in her mouth, yet it was enough to rouse Jamie, who looked up, confused at what she saw.

One more swing. Tony knew he only had one more chance. He had almost dropped the box and could not afford to miss it again. He sank deep into his restraints as he pushed off once more. His shoulder tore, the pain in it going beyond the cramp and acid build up. Tony gritted his teeth and twisted on the rope. He needed his hands to grab the device.

He felt it, cold and solid in his hands, and his fingers closed around it. His arc ended, and his body began to move back. The box slipped in his grip and for a heart-stopping moment, he was sure the device would fall, and it would be over. Adjusting his grip, he quickly snatched at the box and held it fast, dragging it with him as he fell back, swinging like a pendulum.

Tony swung back and forth, his mind so focused on pressing the button to lower him that he did not even think to stop his sway, despite the rampaging pain in his arms.

His thumb found the button and with a surprisingly quiet grind of gears, the ramp began to lower. With his feet firmly on the floor, Tony found the pressure in his arms lessened and freed up his entire body. Stopping the ramp as soon as he could, he worried at his restraints, working at them furiously. Knots had always fascinated him. They were, in many ways, a puzzle that he could solve; which strand to pull, which ones tightened. They were an interwoven puzzle that could occupy his mind for hours when he was younger. Now, with his life on the line, his mind picked apart the knot in seconds.

The moment he was free, he ran toward Stella and Jamie, who were both crying with delight at his closeness.

Tony hurriedly freed Stella and his sister. Jamie tried to speak, but her words were drowned out by the savage bellow that erupted in the street outside.

It was followed by a heavy crash and the sound of splintering wood.

"They're here," Stella said.

"We need a car. We need to escape," Tony replied, not thinking about the creatures that waited for them. His mind was set on getting them to safety, and the best way to do that was with a car.

"We can't go out there," Jamie shrieked, jumping as if being hauled out of a bad dream.

"You stay here. I'll take a look," Tony offered.

"Don't go out there," Stella called after him.

Gunfire sounded in the street close by, the heavy boom of a shotgun. It was followed by another roar that held Tony in place. He looked back over his shoulder. Jamie was hugging Stella, her face buried in her friend's neck.

Tony swallowed, his mouth suddenly dry.

Screams echoed in the street, and the shotgun fired again. It was followed by a burst of automatic gunfire. Someone ran past the garage and passed within a few feet of where they stood, but they were so lost to the throes of blind panic, they did not seem to notice Tony standing there.

A few seconds later, a tree trunk flew through the air crashing into the wall of the garage, decapitating the person that had been in flight mode just seconds before. Their head bounced off the wall and disappeared beneath the uprooted tree.

Tony watched on as he traced the flight path of the tree and found himself staring into the frenzied yellow eyes of a giant cryptid. The creature's gaze was enough to freeze the blood in his veins.

Shotguns barked orders of death and while the first two shots seemed to do little more than irritate the beast, the third strike to its chest opened a fist-sized hole, burrowing deep into the meat. Bright red blood soon covered the creature's chest. Another rattling burst of automatic gunfire turned the beast's face into mincemeat and dropped it to the floor.

Still, it was not dead, but certainly dying. Yet the agonized screams it made would be a beacon to the others that Tony knew waited in the trees. Whether through planning or pure savagery, he didn't know, nor did he care.

"Shut that thing up," a deep voice barked the order.

A barrel-chested man appeared with a beard that dropped down to his chest and a bald head that glistened with bloody sweat. The man carried a large fire ax and wasted no time in hacking away at the creature's neck. Five strong swings and the beast fell silent. Another three, and the head came away from the body in an explosion of blood that showered the executioner with gore.

Tony turned around as the man stood up from its task and stared directly towards him. He needn't panic because before he could sound any alarm, another Bigfoot appeared, charging at the man, tearing his arms from their sockets as if he were made from soft clay rather than skin and bone. The man screamed, flailing with his stumps, showering those that had rushed to his aid with blood.

"We need to move." He hurried back to the girls and took Stella by the hand, leading her and with her, his sister, who still clung to her friend like a limpet. Behind him, the armless man's screams fell silent, but the dogs of war were growling.

They moved to the back of the garage where a fire exit door offered them a chance at freedom.

"Hold on, Jamie," Tony said as he shouldered the door and tumbled out into the back alley that ran adjacent to the main street.

Screams were heavy in the air, drifting towards them from all directions. The stench of impending death hung heavy over the town.

"This way." Tony led them forward, choosing to move away from the garage, continuing in the direction they had been going before they got attacked.

The alley was cramped and overgrown, littered with waist-high wrecks, broken pallets, and general items of debris. A rusty bike frame jabbed at Tony's knee, but his jeans managed to protect him from all but a slight scratch.

They followed the alley for as long as they could before it left them with a decision to make: Left or right. One way brought them back onto the main street, where the majority of the action seemed to be, while the left-hand option took them deeper into the town and closer to the locals that lived there.

"We need to find a car," Tony insisted, his mind still focused on the one single plan: Escape.

He turned to the right and brought them onto the main street. To their immediate left, a group of armed men fired on a smaller Bigfoot who held aloft the lower half of some poor soul. The upper portion was nowhere to be seen. The men saw them appear and as the creature fell, they turned their hungry rifles on the group.

"Shit, run," Stella screamed.

They turned to head back into the alley, but two more men were closing the gap on them, both covered in the blood of their friend, and their eyes gleaming with the desire to extract revenge on anything and everything they could.

"This way," Tony said, heading back down the main street, toward the garage. They saw two more Bigfoot running through the town, both injured and fleeing, but no doubt a temporary retreat. They were chased by a group of five men armed with automatic weapons that looked as if they belonged in a military arsenal rather than some backwater mountain town.

The trio neared the garage, spared from a hail of pursuing bullets by the emergence of another Bigfoot which hurled the body of a skinny man in dungarees through the air like a dart. He sailed through the air, his mullet flitting in the wind behind him like a cape, before his body embedded itself head first into the side of a shed.

The distraction gave them a few moments to put distance between them and their pursuers, slipping into the gathered crowd. The initial wave of Bigfoot had withdrawn, and the headless body of the first Bigfoot they killed had been set on fire, its body a mountain of flame, which may have served as a warning to the others, but also created a smell that was unparalleled in its stench.

The group ran through the crowd, separating momentarily only to regroup on the other side of the fire. They kept running, back the way they had come, toward the Bigfoot, wherever they were, but the darkness of the trees offered them a moment of respite to put together a new plan of attack.

They reached the house that seemed to mark the border of the town, when the front door opened and the skinny man ran outside, naked save for his boots, his penis pointing him forward while the shotgun in his hands followed suit.

He stared at them for a second before the blank expression he wore turned toward recognition. "Waits a minute," he began, pulling his shotgun tight into his bony shoulder.

He never got the chance to pull the trigger because a large fist slammed down onto his head, pushing it down onto, and through, his shoulders like a hammer pounding a nail into a piece of balsa wood. His eyes burst from his skull from the sudden change in pressure and his eardrums burst to send thick gouts of brain matter flying in both directions. Blood flowed from his nose and eyes, and while his body fell lifeless and limp to the floor, his penis remained standing, a testament to his strong sexual constitution.

The scream that followed the assault caused both the trio and the Bigfoot to turn and stare at the house. The fat woman had stumbled into the doorway, her many rolls of flesh open and bare for the world to see, her sagging breasts flowing over and to the side of her large stomach. She looked at her dead man and screamed again, while the Bigfoot looked at her form and cocked its head to the side before it turned and disappeared back into the trees.

The woman turned on the three, advancing on them with steps that set her entire body quivering. Her face darkened to a shade of purple, looking more like a nasty bruise. Tony stood before the women, but they turned to run and found themselves staring down the barrels of half a dozen rifles, the eyes of the men holding them, glaring at them, each one as clear to read as the previous. They were ready to kill them.

"You've gone and caused a real mess. You've upset them and look what happened," Gus, the shopkeeper, said.

"Us?" Stella asked, panting.

"You should have stayed at the cabin. If you'd have stayed in the cabin, then this wouldn't have happened," the mechanic said, his cheeks red with fatigue, his clothes red with blood.

"What are we gonna do with them?" another man asked, his face wiry, etched deep with the lines of a life lived outdoors.

"Kill them. Kill them all. They did this, they killed my Billy. They killed my Billy," the fat woman shrieked. She had fallen to the floor, cradling her dead lover, a position that made her look as well as sound more like a pig than before. She stared at the trio, strands of saliva hanging from her jowls, a feral intensity burning in her eyes.

Looking at the woman, Tony was sure that she would tear them apart on the spot if she had been able to stand quick enough.

He didn't like the woman. It wasn't her size or the way she had been screaming, but he could sense that there was something off about her; something rotten on the inside. He tried to figure everything out and the pieces of the puzzle that held her image were wet and soggy, and they refused to fit into any of the places that were meant for them.

Rough hands grabbed him, the girls too. They were dragged back toward the garage, pulled roughly and led in the middle of a cavalcade of armed men. They were marched into the town, close by the burning Bigfoot. The flames had cut through the mass of fur on his body and found the real flesh beneath. The smell of roasting meat was a tainted one, carried on the back of the stench of burning fur. Tony's stomach rolled, and he wanted to vomit.

The trio was brought into the garage once more, but instead of being tied up, there were taken into the office area, and through that into a small supply closet, barely big enough to hold two people with all the shelves and boxes that filled it. Crammed inside, they were plunged into a total darkness as the door slammed shut and locked, sealing them inside.

Tony stood pressed against the wall, a box of something jabbing into the small of his back. Stella stood pressed up against him, her near-naked body cold and shivering. Beside her, Jamie still clung to her friend, a broken shell of who she had been. Her body trembled, not with cold but with shock. Tony wanted to tell her it would be okay, to try and soothe her mind the way she had helped him over the years. He just did not know how. He jumped when he felt something crawling around his waist, but relaxed when he realized it was Stella, wrapping her arms around him. She held him tight, squeezing him even, and Tony didn't want her to stop. In the darkness, he smiled.

CHAPTER THIRTEEN

The clamor of voices rose until it was an indistinguishable din. Gus stood at the head of the group with Hank beside him. The pair had been in charge of the guard committee for almost thirty years, taking over the roles from their fathers and their fathers before them. They knew what needed to be done. All sense of order had been lost. The Bigfoot were angry and had every right to be.

"This ends tonight," Gus said, his voice authoritative, cutting through the din and silencing everybody in the room.

The chatter settled down and everybody turned to face the pair.

"They should have died tonight, but there is still time. The beasts are angry, but we fought them back. They know their rightful place. They will be fed tonight, the same way they have been fed for centuries." His words held the crowd, who listened to what he had to say as if he were some revered speaker dishing out must-hear life advice.

"They need to die for what they did to my Billy," the fat woman squealed once again. She sat at the back of the room, a large sheet held around her body. Her dirt-covered face was streaked with the tears she had shed.

"Easy now, Mae. They have a lot to answer for, but the beasts must be appeased. They need to feed. You all know how this works. We feed them, they stay in the hills and protect us from what lives above them. It's not a matter of revenge, but of duty. My great-great-grandfather was the first to keep the watch, and I will not sully his name by failing now," Gus spoke, staring at Mae, but taking in the looks of everybody that faced them.

"Kill them and leave them in the woods," a voice shouted from the pack.

"Now, hold on. It's not that simple, damnit. The beasts like them alive. They like fresh meat. Now, in all these years, they've only ever come to town twice before tonight. Both times our ancestors fought them off. Send them back to the woods." Gus tried to settle the group, to strip away the anger and get down to the reality.

"Y'all saw it for yourselves. There's more of 'em than we realized, and who knows how many there could be still up there. We need to play it smart. Keep them happy and keep everybody safe. The secret of the mountains is more important than us, and you know it. I know we lost people tonight, family and friends alike, but we have our duty," Hank said, taking over the conversation, his words firmer if not less compulsive to the ears.

"Now, listen up. Frank, you take your boys and clear out the streets. Doc and the Reverend are waiting for you. We'll bury our dead at dawn, but they can't stay where they are now. Hank, take a couple of guys and bring 'em to the woods. Go as far as you can, tie 'em up, and leave 'em there. The beasts will find them. You can be sure of that." Gus ran through the list of tasks like a site foreman starting a new build project. He dished out the orders, and everybody nodded. At the end of the day, they all knew their place and accepted the tasks handed to them, even those that were told to go home and stay out of the way.

The meeting ended and most people filtered out and went about their tasks. Only Mae remained sitting, waiting until the room was empty before approaching Gus.

"They need to die, Gus. You know it." She stared at him, her eyes burning pink with tears.

"They will die, sure as the sun will rise tomorrow. It just won't be by your hand, Mae. Trust me, this is how it needs to be." Gus placed a hand on her mammoth shoulder. "Now, I'll hear no more of it, you understand."

Mae looked him in the eyes and nodded, slowly. "What am I going to do? I can't be alone." Tears brimmed in her eyes, a fresh wave of pain at the concept of a lonely future.

Gus was quiet for a moment, lowering his head in thought. He let out a long, slow breath. "Go home. Back home, to Ma and Pa. You can stay there tonight, and we'll figure something out in the morning."

"You always knew how to take care of me, big brother," Mae said, smiling. She turned and walked away, leaving the two champions standing tall.

"You know what needs to be done." Gus looked at Hank who nodded. "Do it."

Gus walked away and out into the town. He had other things to attend to.

It was hot and airless in the small back room. Tony was sticky with sweat, and while he had come to relish the closeness of Stella's body, it brought with it a nervousness he had not experienced before. Her every touch, every breath he took tasted of her, and it only served to make his nerves dance even more.

The door opened and the rush of cool air against his skin felt great, but Jamie's scream brought everything back. Hauled from the closet, Stella and Tony followed. The mechanic stood there, a shotgun in his hands. "One move and I'll shoot you," he growled.

"You can't. I heard what that man said," Stella bit back, a defiant streak rising up inside of her.

The fat man looked her up and down and then laughed. "I never said I'd kill you. But if I take off a leg, well, that blood is going to get them all riled up."

The words had a chilling finality to them, and Stella felt her defiance die down, wilting as if a bucket of ice water had been thrown over her head.

They were marched at gunpoint out of the office and back into the garage, the blood-stained floor a stark reminder of what they had already lost. Outside, the corpse still burned, although the flames had eaten through a lot of their food supply. A breeze was blowing the smoke away from the town, but right into the trees, where it would surely only anger the Bigfoot that had survived.

Pushed into the street, there were three other men waiting for them. Each had a length of rope and secured the trio's arms behind their backs.

As they reached the rear of the broken-down pick-up, an almighty roar reverberated around the town. It wasn't a single sound, created by a single set of beastly lungs, but rather a cry bellowed by a pack. It was a declaration of war as easy to understand as anything in the world.

"Shit, you hear that?" one of the three men asked.

"Get 'em in the damned truck," Hank growled, giving Jamie a shove so she fell against the lowered tailgate.

The men pushed Tony and the girls into the trunk and slammed the back shut. They slapped the side panel as a sign that their task was done, and the engine growled into life.

Tony lay on the bed of the truck, his arms tied, and his mind clogged with problems. If they could get the truck, they could escape. But there was no way of taking it. Not now. They were being driven back towards *them*, and it would be too late. He felt the edges of panic creeping over him. Slow deep breaths fought against it for a time, but it was a trick that could not work forever.

When the truck first lurched to one side, he thought they had hit one of the potholes in the road, or perhaps merely run straight over one of the corpses that littered the street. When it happened a second time, and he heard the driver curse, he realized that something was wrong.

There was a crash and suddenly the truck not only lurched and leaped into the air, it tilted to the left, rolling the group in the bed against the siding. Tony was crushed by the sudden weight of both Stella and his sister. The truck continued to rise, and just as it began to flip, they were thrown from the bed and dumped onto the hard ground.

Pain flared in Tony's shoulder, and his head bounced off the road hard enough for him to see stars, but he fought to remain conscious. The truck completed its rotation and came to a rest upside-down, the passenger-side caved in from where the boulder had been hurled into it.

The world around him exploded It sounded as though a jet engine was taking off and they were trapped not near it, but within it. The noise came from everywhere, assaulting them from all sides as the Bigfoot closed ranks.

They came from everywhere, their bodies dropping from the trees as if spawned there. Five appeared close to where they were and tore at the truck, ripping it apart and using the pieces as missiles they launched into the town.

Tony threw himself flat on the ground when he saw the group of beasts turn and start their advance on the town. "Stay down," he yelled at Stella and his sister.

The Bigfoot swept past them and joined the others that had swept in from the sides. Buildings were trashed, and debris soon littered the streets. The now-familiar background music of gunfire rattled.

"They're everywhere," Stella screamed as she looked around for a place they could head.

"We need to move," Tony said, his mind still focused on finding a car. "This way."

Tony led them away from the main intersection, where the core conflict seemed to be underway, and hurried down a smaller street, disappearing around the side of the first house they came to. There were no lights on and the building looked to be in terrible condition. The front door was unlocked, and they charged inside, eager for the brief respite from the crazy affair playing out outside.

The stench in the house was foul, but nothing compared to the general odor of the Bigfoot. Tony slammed the door shut behind them and turned to lean against it. He gasped when he saw the two skeletal figures staring at them. Sitting only a few meters away from them, he mistook them for the dead at first. It was only when one started wagging its jaw up and down as if sounding a silent alarm that he realized they were both alive.

The pair sat in wheelchairs, their bodies covered by ratty blankets. A general aroma of piss and shit emanated from them, while there were several trays of half-eaten meals strewn over the floor, each one in various stages of rot. Maggots crawled all over one plate in particular, their swollen yellow bodies overflowing onto the floor.

"Oh my God, they're alive," Stella gasped, the realization dawning on her a little later. Jamie said nothing but gave a muffled scream.

Turning to his sister, Tony saw that she was not even looking at the two elderly figures, but rather the obese frame that filled the doorway. The angry woman from earlier stood with a plate of food in one hand, while her other was halfway to her crumb-coated mouth. She gazed at the three and dropped the plate, which shattered on the floor. Stumbling backward, she disappeared into the kitchen.

"Get out of this house! You did this! Look at what you did!" She disappeared for a moment, but her high-pitched accusations continued. When she reemerged, the plate had been replaced by an old-school double barrel.

Tony jumped forward at the sight of the gun. The woman was struggling against her bulk to turn both the weapon and her body to face her targets. Tony grabbed the gun with both hands and wrestled it away from the woman, whose shrieks had turned into pig-like squeals, as though she were suffering from some unprovoked attack.

With the gun in his possession, Tony backed up, while the woman continued to scream. Caught in the doorway, she had but one direction to go. She took several shuddering steps toward them when the shotgun boomed and her stomach burst, showering the wall with a vast spray of red. Her shrieks stopped as the woman looked down at the blossoming flower of meat that was rising up through the hole in the sheet that was still wrapped around her body. She began to shake, her enormous body quivering for a few moments, while blood started to drip from her rolling flesh like rain. Without making another sound, she dropped to the floor, landing face first in the maggot-infested plate.

"I didn't mean to," Tony said shocked. He held the gun at arm's length, as if he didn't trust it not to turn on him next.

"It's okay. You had to." Stella's voice was a weight that cut through the panic that Tony felt. He turned towards her, fighting off the urge to cry.

"We need to keep moving," she said, grabbing blindly behind her for Jamie's hand.

"We need to find a car," Tony repeated. It had become his mantra for survival, the one notion that he held true and unwavering in his mind. If they found a car, they would be safe.

The gunfire continued to rage outside, and a crash from close by told them that the Bigfoot were still at large.

"There has to be a back door," Tony said, moving into the house, stepping over the mammoth legs of the dead woman. The room behind was a kitchen, small and sweaty, a cesspit of the highest order. Dirty plates and cups were stacked in haphazard piles, and a sink blocked by something given the still water that sat in it.

"Here," Tony said, following another small hallway into a back room that was lined from floor to ceiling with newspapers and other items of memorabilia that held no value or importance.

The door was partially blocked, but Tony had no desire to leave the house as they found it, and so with Stella's help, they pushed over the pile of newspapers which crumbled partially to dust that their touch.

To their surprise, Jamie opened the door and fell into the cool-by-comparison air. The backyard was just as much of a mess as inside the house, but they had an uninhibited escape route and were soon running in single file down the alleyway that separated the rows of housing.

They reached the end of the alley and turned to the right. A Bigfoot turned to meet them, its yellow eyes burning like fires. It opened its mouth and roared, revealing its blood-stained teeth

Tony stumbled and fumbled with the shotgun. He took aim and fired but missed his target by some margin. The creature's head exploded nonetheless, however, as the volley of fire that came from behind tore its thick skull apart.

The trio didn't wait to see who had inadvertently saved them but continued running. They crossed the street and ducked inside another building, a shop of some description, but they paid it no attention as they ran through and out of the front door.

Back on the main street, they couldn't avoid the townsfolk, but one look told them that they were no longer a major concern. The street was filled with Bigfoot. Tony guessed at least twenty, with more most likely waiting to move in. Three houses were ablaze, and as they watched, the burning figure of a large beast emerged through the wall, making it several meters before collapsing to the floor under a burst of heavy gunfire.

The townsfolk were putting up a good fight, but for each Bigfoot they claimed, they lost at least three people in return. Bodies lay everywhere, few of them whole. Blood flowed in the street like a river, and body parts lay scattered all over the place, like discarded shoes by the side of a motorway.

Tony's mind exploded from the input, but he forced away the puzzles and the need to sort it out. It was all bad, plain and simple.

"There. The store." He pointed down the street to the store, the place where their adventure had begun.

Running, trying their best to dodge the bullets that were flying all around them, they headed to the store.

Inside, it was cool and dark. The smell that had been so noticeable when they first visited was nothing now. At best, they could tell the store was empty. Somewhere out back, something heavy crashed, but nothing else seemed to be inside with them.

They relaxed for a moment.

"I'll grab something to drink. We need water," Stella said as Tony took a moment to close his eyes.

Stella disappeared into the store in search of water, leaving Tony and his sister by the register.

"You alright?" Tony asked, looking at Jamie. She had said very little since the cabin and seemed to be disappearing inside herself. Her arms were permanently clamped around her own torso when she wasn't being led from one place to another.

Jamie looked up at him and nodded, but Tony saw it in her eyes that she was lying. Her green eyes that had once been so bright were now muted, like the murky color of the sea. Part of Jamie had died up at the cabin, and not just because of Colin.

Tony moved over to his sister and put his arms around her. She seemed to melt into him, vanishing from the world.

There was another crash in the store, the sound of goods falling from the shelves. Tony spun around but couldn't see anything. Then Stella appeared, carrying several bottles of water. Her eyes were wide, and she stared at Tony, biting her bottom lip. She stopped and then Gus appeared, emerging from the shadows, rifle in hand and a crazed look in his eyes.

"You done gone messed it all up," he spoke, his voice wavering, like a man balancing on the edge of his own sanity.

"We didn't do anything. They just attacked us up at the cabin. The cabin you sent us to," Tony said, moving in front of his sister while alternating his stare between the crazy man with the gun and Stella.

"That's the point. You were there for them. You need to feed the beast," the man spat pure fury and white foam flew from his lips. "For generations, we have kept them happy. Kept them in the woods. But now... Now you've done it. There is a purpose for everything. We all have our duty, and yours was to die in the woods." The man let go of Stella as he clamped a hand against the side of his head.

Stella ran at Tony, collapsing into his arms.

"You're crazy," Tony said.

"Crazy? Crazy? Fuck you, I'm not crazy. I'm doing my duty. The way my pa and grandpa and grandpa before him did. My family has always kept watch over the beasts, and they kept watch over us in return. Don't you understand? Don't you see? The secret of the mountains, it's coming now, and we can't stop it." The man returned his gaze to the group, but his face had changed. His eyes were unfocused as if something inside of him had broken.

"You killed us all." He stared at them. "But maybe it's not too late. Maybe I can still end this. Move," he ordered, walking toward the store's entrance.

Something crashed on the roof, shaking the store to its foundations.

It was that, more than Gus, that got them moving. Jamie whimpered but said nothing as they backed up into the street.

The fight was dying down. The townsfolk were low on numbers, but the Bigfoot seemed to be less also. There was a rumble in the ground, a vibration that seemed to carry through the entire town. Everything shook with it. Even the blood river rippled like a pond in the breeze.

Gus stood in the entrance to his shop, his gun lowered. He wasn't going to kill them. He needed them alive as a peace offering for the beasts.

"We're going to end this now," he said, trying to force a confident authoritative tone into his words, but failing. Like a child trying to stand up to the school bully, his words meant well but sounded tinny and ineffective.

The long arm came from nowhere, dropping down from the sky. The hand closed around Gus's head, and with what looked to be a gentle movement, plucked it from the body, the way you would pull a strawberry from the plant.

His body spasmed, his finger squeezing the trigger of his rifle, and a burst of wild bullets sprayed around them. The group flinched and ducked, turning away from the body as the fountain of blood shot into the air from the severed stump that had been its neck.

They didn't see the Bigfoot, or where it went once it had claimed the prize, but the inevitable assault they expected did not come.

Suddenly, there was silence around them. Even the air was cold and dead. The streets were littered with the bodies of the dead, from both sides. Big and small, whole and dismembered, they were mixed together; side by side, the casualties of war.

The three friends stood in the center of the road and looked around them. The town was in ruins. The fires that had started were spreading, the ramshackle buildings catching like dry kindling. Smoke blackened their air which was darkening, swelling with the threat of another storm.

"Do you feel that?" Stella asked.

"What is it?" Tony asked in return. "It's like when the subway rushes by under your feet."

"There's no subway out here," Jamie spoke, her voice light and airy. Before the others could say anything else, she collapsed in the street, blood pooling around her.

"Jamie!" Tony cried, grabbing at his sister, trying to catch her even after she had hit the ground. "Jamie!"

Jamie lay on the cold concrete and opened her eyes. She looked up at her brother, one of the best people she knew. She smiled. It was all she could think of doing. Her body was cold. She felt so cold. It reminded her of the time she had jumped into the lake at the start of spring. A whole group of them had done it. None of them expected it to be as cold as it was. This was worse. She could feel it spreading through her, dulling the burning ache in her gut from where the stray bullet had torn her open.

She could feel her body pulsing, forcing more blood through the wound that she tried so hard to hold closed. She could also feel it lessening, as her body slowly shut down.

"I love you, Tony," she stuttered, her tongue betraying her, strangling her final words.

Tony cried. Thick heavy tears streamed from his face. He didn't speak. He couldn't. Jamie couldn't take the pain in his eyes, so looked away. "Stella." Her voice was now a whisper.

"Yes," Stella sniffed out through her own tears.

"Look after him." The words were barely out of Jamie's mouth before the darkness swarmed in, overtaking her in a flood, like a drowning man finally opening his mouth and letting the water take him.

For a few moments, neither of them moved. They knelt by Jamie's body, another victim to the town of death that surrounded them.

"We need to leave," Stella said, her voice broken and raw.

"No," Tony said, clutching at his sister.

"Tony, look at me." The words didn't register. "Tony."

Stella reached out and took Tony's hand in her own. She stood up and Tony came with her, following her movements. She turned him around and looked him in the eyes. "I love you, Tony, and we need to move now if we are going to escape this place."

Tony nodded. Not in agreement, or because he had even heard what she had said, but because it was the only response there was to give.

There was a beat-up pick-up truck in the far corner of the parking lot. The windows were broken, and it looked to have seen better days, but as long as it started, then it would be good enough.

Moving slowly, their bodies numb, the pair moved arm in arm toward the truck. There was something on the ground beside it: Hank's severed head. It was battered and bruised, but undeniably that of the fat mechanic. Stella stared at it, before pulling back her foot and kicking it across the parking lot.

"Motherfucker," she screamed at the rolling cranium. Her foot hurt, but she felt a little better for having done it.

They climbed into the truck together, and after finding the keys hidden in the sun visor, they both said a silent prayer and tried the engine.

It caught at the third time of asking, barking a rusty cough and spluttering before the engine steadied out.

Pulling out of the lot, eager to put as much distance as they could between them and the town, they froze. The street was filled with Bigfoot. Not the dozen or so that had survived the battle, but hundreds of them. From large to tiny, infants smaller than they were, they filled the town like a flood overrunning everything. They lined the buildings and stood tall on various roofs that remained standing, the fires providing an ominous and eerie backdrop to the scene. Tony pressed his foot even harder against the floor, and his hands clamped down on the wheel. He didn't realize he had been holding his breath until his lungs started to burn.

"What do you think that man meant?" Stella asked, her eyes focus on the wing mirror, watching the town grow smaller and smaller behind them.

"What do you mean?" Tony asked, his eyes focused on the road.

"When he said the Bigfoot were protecting them as much as they protected it?" Stella stared at the scene and thought she saw something behind the town, some vast shape forming in the gloom, rising up against the stormy sky. Invisible and massive, it formed within the smoke and clouds. She shuddered as a cold chill ran through her.

"Nothing. They were all crazy," Tony replied, tears streaking his cheeks.

Stella looked back again, but the town was behind them now, and the sky looked as any other stormy afternoon sky would look.

"I guess. What do we do now?" Stella asked as she placed her hand on Tony's atop the gear stick.

"Now we go home." Tony looked at Stella and smiled. "We go home."

THE END

SEVEREDPRESS

f facebook.com/severedpress
🐦 twitter.com/severedpress

CHECK OUT OTHER GREAT HORROR NOVELS

DEATH CRAWLERS
by Gerry Griffiths

Worldwide, there are thought to be 8,000 species of centipede, of which, only 3,000 have been scientifically recorded. The venom of Scolopendra gigantea—the largest of the arthropod genus found in the Amazon rainforest—is so potent that it is fatal to small animals and toxic to humans. But when a cargo plane departs the Amazon region and crashes inside a national park in the United States, much larger and deadlier creatures escape the wreckage to roam wild, reproducing at an astounding rate. Entomologist, Frank Travis solicits small town sheriff Wanda Rafferty's help and together they investigate the crash site. But as a rash of gruesome deaths befalls the townsfolk of Prospect, Frank and Wanda will soon discover how vicious and cunning these new breed of predators can be. Meanwhile, Jake and Nora Carver, and another backpacking couple, are venturing up into the mountainous terrain of the park. If only they knew their fun-filled weekend is about to become a living nightmare.

THE PULLER
by Michael Hodges

Matt Kearns has two choices: fight or hide. The creature in the orchard took the rest. Three days ago, he arrived at his favorite place in the world, a remote shack in Michigan's Upper Peninsula. The plan was to mourn his father's death and figure out his life. Now he's fighting for it. An invisible creature has him trapped. Every time Matt tries to flee, he's dragged backwards by an unseen force. Alone and with no hope of rescue, Matt must escape the Puller's reach. But how do you free yourself from something you cannot see?

SEVEREDPRESS

🅕 facebook.com/severedpress

🅧 twitter.com/severedpress

CHECK OUT OTHER GREAT HORROR NOVELS

BLACK FRIDAY
by Michael Hodges

Jared the kleptomaniac, Chike the unemployed IT guy, Patricia the shopaholic, and Jeff the meth dealer are trapped inside a Chicago supermall on Black Friday. Bridgefield Mall empties during a fire alarm, and most of the shoppers drive off into a strange mist surrounding the mall parking lot. They never return. Chike and his group try calling friends and family, but their smart phones won't work, not even Twitter. As the mist creeps closer, the mall lights flicker and surge. Bulbs shatter and spray glass into the air. Unsettling noises are heard from within the mist, as the meth dealer becomes unhinged and hunts the group within the mall. Cornered by the mist, and hunted from within, Chike and the survivors must fight for their lives while solving the mystery of what happened to Bridgefield Mall. Sometimes, a good sale just isn't worth it.

GRIMWEAVE
by Tim Curran

In the deepest, darkest jungles of Indochina, an ancient evil is waiting in a forgotten, primeval valley. It is patient, monstrous, and bloodthirsty. Perfectly adapted to its hot, steaming environment, it strikes silent and stealthy, it chosen prey: human. Now Michael Spiers, a Marine sniper, the only survivor of a previous encounter with the beast, is going after it again. Against his better judgement, he is made part of a Marine Force Recon team that will hunt it down and destroy it.

The hunters are about to become the hunted.

www.ingramcontent.com/pod-product-compliance
Lightning Source LLC
Chambersburg PA
CBHW052002170626
46808CB00007B/2732